Plantagenet Embers
Novellas

Stories of

Margaret Beaufort
Elizabeth Woodville
&
Reginald Pole

Books by Samantha Wilcoxson

Luminous: The Story of a Radium Girl

The Plantagenet Embers Trilogy

Plantagenet Princess, Tudor Queen: The Story of Elizabeth of York
Faithful Traitor: The Story of Margaret Pole
Queen of Martyrs: The Story of Mary I

Middle Grade Fiction

Over the Deep: A Titanic Adventure
No Such Thing as Perfect

Plantagenet Embers Novellas

The Last Lancastrian: A Story of Margaret Beaufort
Once a Queen: A Story of Elizabeth Woodville
Prince of York: A Story of Reginald Pole

Samantha Wilcoxson

Paperback ISBN-10: 1723364983
Paperback ISBN-13: 978-1723364983
Hardcover ISBN: 9798544305828

The Last Lancastrian

A Story of Margaret Beaufort

Samantha Wilcoxson

To all the mothers who would do anything for their sons.

July 1469

Margaret forced the tension from her shoulders and concentrated on smoothing the deep furrows from her brow. Releasing a breath and straightening her back, she refocused her mind upon her prayers. The coolness of the stone floor felt refreshing compared to the sticky summer day, but Margaret scarcely noticed.

She knelt before the altar frustrated that she could not do more. She accepted both gifts and the trials from God and had received many of both, but how she wished that he would make a way for her to be with her son. Could she trust anyone else to protect him with their very life, the way she would?

On the other hand, she thought, which of those men, so sure of themselves in battle, would go before the throne of God with her fervency on Henry's behalf? None. She allowed herself a slight smile. Her work was the most vital, and she would see it done well.

Shifting on her thin knees for slightly improved comfort, Margaret prepared for her charge.

~ ~ ~ ~

News of the recent battle created a vile blend of emotions within Margaret that caused her stomach to churn and made her head feel faint. A hand placed on her narrow waist did not alleviate the nausea that followed the knowledge that her son had been in battle – and on the losing side.

"How could he?" she raged against William Herbert. He, of course, was not present, but the disheveled messenger stood as his proxy. She knew that she could not truly blame Herbert for taking his twelve-year-old ward into battle. It was the only way Henry would learn to fight, but, as she wondered if her son had escaped the bloody field alive, Margaret did indeed blame him very much.

Suddenly realizing that the messenger remained awkwardly

before her, Margaret waved him away. He fled with thankful speed from the tiny woman whose rage was as fierce as any man's. Margaret did not waste another thought upon him. She was already contemplating her own rescue mission.

Her wine-colored skirts swayed with the rhythm of her quick steps and filled the air with the fragrance of lavender from the rushes. Margaret could not be still as her mind worked, so she paced with fervent motion.

Surely, God would not be cruel enough to take her only son from her, nor ironic enough to have him die in the service of the York king, Edward IV. Margaret shivered at the possibility, because she could not quite convince herself that it did not exist.

Within minutes, William Bailey was at her side, discussing her plans. Focusing on practical matters soothed Margaret's fears, occupied her mind, and stilled her nervous energy.

"I trust none more than you to lead the search party," Margaret said, pinning William with an intense gaze that sharpened the compliment. He simply bowed his head in acceptance of the praise and mission, his dark hair shielding his face from her view.

"I would have my best eight men sent to locate Henry," Margaret demanded. "Before nightfall," she added.

With an unnecessary glance at the declining sun and a repressed sigh, William acquiesced with no more protest than an almost imperceptible tightening of his jaw. There was little point in doing anything else, this he knew from years of serving the countess. "I shall see it done," he assured her, sounding more eager than he felt. The men's complaints upon receipt of his orders were already ringing in his ears, but he would fulfill his duty.

"Good," Margaret stated with a firm nod. She gestured toward the door to release him. "I will let you see to it immediately. I expect frequent communication of your progress."

She watched his quick, determined stride, satisfying herself that all would be done according to her will. Pressing her lips into a thin line, she wondered if it would be enough.

Margaret's arms went around herself as she moved to the window, as if she thought she might immediately see horses racing away carrying the men who were tasked with finding her son. Her willowy form had rounded only once with child, and that child was out there somewhere amidst bloodthirsty soldiers who would not hesitate to slay him like any other enemy. How she wished she could go with them and bundle Henry up to bring him home with her.

The corners of her mouth fell further. She was being ridiculous. The very idea of coddling a boy on the cusp of manhood was one that she would not have hesitated to rebuke another for. Yet, here she was, wishing that she was holding him close and running her fingers through his tangled hair.

"Absurd!" she admonished herself, spinning away from the window to find more purposeful work for herself. This idleness and sentimentality would not bring Henry home. She marched out of the chamber toward the kitchen, where she would see that sufficient rations were packed for those preparing to leave.

Within the hour, Margaret stood stiffly, ignoring the beauty of the setting sun to watch the men gallop away to search for her son amidst the debris left in the wake of battle.

Once she could no longer make out their forms in the growing distance and fading light, Margaret moved inside, suddenly aware of the coldness creeping into her limbs. The fire in her rooms had been tended, just as it was each evening. She found that she was always cold at night, regardless of what heat the day had brought. Margaret warmed her hands and allowed herself some small comfort from the golden flames before deciding that there was little hope of sleep that night.

A warm woolen cloak was selected instead of a nightshift,

and Margaret made her way to the chapel to spend the dark hours in prayer for the safety of her son and those she had placed her trust in to locate him.

Her prayers were unceasing for hours before her mind started wandering. Weariness invaded her vigil, and candlelight created curious images upon the chapel's stone walls. Margaret began to wonder at the idea that her son might have been killed fighting for a York king. If it were not a life and death matter, she could have laughed at the idea that one of the few remaining Lancastrian sons might have met his fate supporting Edward IV.

When she was not in torment over the fate of her son, Margaret spared some worry for her husband. He would have been spared fighting Warwick because King Edward's personal forces had not reached the battlefield in time to add their blood to the mix. Yet, Harry was with the York king and may have to fight another day by his side.

Richard Neville, Earl of Warwick, might regret his part in putting York on the throne, but Margaret's family would not risk their lives as part of his rebellion, whatever their deepest loyalties.

Harry would have served Henry VI at a moment's notice, just as his father had, but fighting against Edward was not equivalent to fighting for the Lancastrian king. No, in this battle between cousins, Harry Stafford surprised himself by siding with York.

Realizing that her thoughts were taking her far from God, Margaret slowly rose. The candles had slowly burned down to nubs, and their failing light were being replaced by pink streams of sunlight that struggled to chase away the darkness of night. That hopeful light gave Margaret the reassurance that she could now rest. If her husband and son had survived the night, the day was not a threat.

At a much slower pace than the steps that had carried her to the chapel the evening before, Margaret shuffled her way to her room with her cloak pulled tightly around her. Pausing only long enough to remove her headdress and loosen the most restrictive of her ties, she fell to bed almost fully clothed. Peaceful sleep soon softened the lines of worry that had grown too deep for a woman of Margaret's years.

~ ~ ~ ~

When news slowly filtered across the country to reach Margaret in Surrey, it was not uplifting. The Battle of Edgecote Moor had not gone in King Edward's favor as most everything else in his life had. He had made taking the crown look easy after his father's abysmal failure, but Warwick had now proven what a vital part he had played in Edward's kingmaking.

Could the king's Neville cousin unmake a king as easily as he had made one?

After dismissing the messenger who had brought news of the defeat, Margaret sat unmoving as she considered the paths the future might take. Would Warwick place Edward's brother of Clarence on the throne as his puppet if his rebellion continued victorious? Margaret shook her head in disbelief. All this to trade one York brother for the other? She would assume nothing at this point.

She stood, smoothing her dress and pulling in a deep breath. While the messenger had no news of her husband or son, he had informed her of William Herbert's end. Captured by Warwick's forces, he had been beheaded on the day following the battle. This caused Margaret little reason to mourn since there was no indication that Henry had shared his guardian's fate. On the contrary, Herbert's death opened the opportunity for Margaret to gain custody of Henry. She would not allow her hopes to float too high, because she feared crashing to the ground if the king said no.

Still uncertain of what action to take until she knew more, Margaret's hands fidgeted with her coral rosary beads as she aimlessly paced through rooms and corridors. The pointlessness irritated her, but neither could she bring her mind to focus on any task that might demand her attention. She could think of nothing besides the eight men she had sent and those they had gone to search for.

Turning a sharp corner, Margaret collided with a breathless woman, one of her ladies-in-waiting. "In the hall," she managed to squeak out before Margaret raced away.

The sight of her own livery, dusty and dirty from hard riding, made a lump rise in Margaret's throat rather than give her comfort, but she did not slow her pace. Not knowing was far worse than receiving bad tidings. Before William stood from his bow, she demanded his story.

"Your son is alive," he began, knowing this was the most important information he had to impart. He was rewarded with an immediate softening in Margaret's features as she closed her eyes and gave thanks to God for protecting Henry.

After a few silent moments, Margaret opened her eyes and nodded for William to continue. Her thin hands remained clutched tightly together.

"He has been taken to safety at Weobley, but Pembroke and Devon have both been executed. Earl Rivers and his son, John, have been taken prisoner."

Margaret looked for the closest seat. The earl of Devon, her husband's brother, was dead. She had not even considered that possibility. Warwick had been more successful than she could have imagined. What did he propose to do with the queen's father and brother in hand?

"Who sees to Henry?" she asked the more important question.

"He is in the care of the Lady Anne. It seemed prudent to have him remain there."

Margaret was already nodding her agreement. She could not hope to have greater access to her son by taking it when it had not been granted. Herbert's widow was capable enough, and Henry's safety was more important than her desires.

"I cannot have him brought here, but I can see to his needs," Margaret replied, already gesturing for her chamberlain. "He should have anything he requires," she ordered. Her look between the two men said that she would leave determining those requirements to them.

She left William to refresh himself and gather what he would for her son. As she made her way to her chamber, her stride slowed as the weariness of the past days finally crashed down upon her. The anxiety and need for action leaving her now that Henry was safe, Margaret came to a halt in the middle of the empty corridor. Leaning against the wall with no one to hold her, she released the tears that she had been holding back.

It seemed silly to cry now, when she finally knew that Henry was safe. The more she inwardly chided herself, the heavier her sobs became. Pent up fears, momentary joy, and concern for the unknown future welled up in her eyes and overflowed.

Allowing herself only a few minutes of emotional release, Margaret rubbed roughly at her reddened eyes and continued to her room. The men would adequately see to Henry's needs, but she wished to offer him a mother's comfort and encouragement. She wanted him to know that he was loved and that she desired nothing more than to be with him. What gift could relay that message?

Margaret scanned the contents of her trunks and shelves, but she became frustrated with the effort. She slammed down the lid of the chest she was searching and turned to sit upon it. Her head rested in her hands as she gave herself an additional moment to wallow in uncharacteristic self-pity. What did God mean by this? She had worked to build bonds with the York regime only for the sake of her son. What would happen if King Edward was deposed?

She wanted to scream.

Instead, she closed her eyes and talked herself out of her pit. It did no good to dwell in dark thoughts. Taking a deep breath, she stood, straight and thin as an arrow. She would trust God's plan.

Turning once again to her books, one caught her eye that she knew was perfect for Henry. The tiny book of hours contained illuminations that were expertly done, both beautiful and filled with clever details. As Margaret fingered the pages, a smile lifted her lips when she imagined Henry's appreciation of them. Margaret loved the vivid colors accompanying each page's prayer, especially the gold that shimmered as though with life of its own. She lovingly caressed the cover as she closed it and set it aside for her son.

By the time she handed a bundle to add to the supplies gathered for Henry, she was composed and appeared confident of her future. When Henry opened the package to find a thick wool cloak, blue horse blanket, and the tiny book of hours with a note inside from his mother, he would have no way of knowing that Margaret ever experienced doubt or sorrow.

Watching the party ride away once again to deliver the goods to Weobley, Margaret still wished that she could go. It was her burden to remain where no one needed her while others saw to the care of her son. Her jawline stiffened and her chin went up without her realizing she did so. Henry was alive. It was more than could be said of many men, so she refused to give in to despair.

She turned in a swirl of skirts and made her way to her study. Maybe she would not be the one to personally order Henry's life, but she would see that his future was one that he deserved. In her mind, she was already composing the letters to her husband and others close to the king. All would know that her son had valiantly fought for King Edward IV. She could only hope that one day he would be rewarded for his loyalty.

August 1469

Margaret was thankful that Harry had arrived shortly following the departure of the group sent to her son. Her husband's easy-going personality smoothed her hard edges and softened her intensity just by being present. Harry had never berated her for failing to give him a son of his own and loved Henry as much as any stepfather could. He was amiably riding at her side as they made their way to London to negotiate for custody of the only child they would ever have.

And they would visit Henry.

Margaret was anxious to see for herself that he was completely unharmed, to look into his eyes and confirm that the haunted look worn by so many men who survived battles was not present in the countenance of her twelve-year-old son. As their caravan traipsed toward London, Margaret did not share her husband's wonder for the natural beauty that he attempted to point out and share with her. Her vision was filled with the image of a tall, gangly boy who shared her hazel eyes and glimmer of Plantagenet red in his hair.

"Margaret, another man would accuse his wife of having a clandestine love should he receive so little attention as your poor spouse."

Harry's words were rounded out with laughter as he reached to stroke her arm. She broke from her inner thoughts to offer him an apologetic grin.

"I do get lost in the world of my own mind," she admitted. "Forgive me, Harry, for I am a poor traveling companion this day."

He gave her a playful pinch before allowing their horses to return to a more comfortable distance apart. "You will think of a way of making it up to me," he assured her with a wink.

"Oh, Harry," she sighed. Margaret was thankful for his forgiving nature but was not in the mood for flirtation. She could not separate herself from the task at hand the way he could.

Thankfully, the spires of the churches of London were beginning to pierce the horizon. The smile she beamed at Harry told him she expected her mission to be a success. She did not expect him to say anything, so any doubts he held were kept to himself.

Once they were settled into their luxurious rooms, Harry eased himself into a cushioned chair with a mug of spirits strong enough for Margaret to smell from across the room. Her brows came together and lips disappeared into a fine line. They had more important things to do during their time in the city than relax.

Then, she noticed a subtle quake in the hand that held the cup and imagined the sores that the long ride had likely caused to open along his legs. Harry was not one to complain, but Margaret knew that the skin affliction he hid from others could sometimes cause him great pain. She released her anger and went to her husband.

Kneeling before him, she asked, "Can I fetch your poultice?" A gentle hand on his knee told him that she worried about his health.

With a relieved sigh, Harry waved away her ministrations. "Just to rest here a bit and look upon my lovely wife is all I need," he insisted.

Margaret shook her head and scoffed. She knew that she was many things, but that a beauty was not one of them. However, she was thankful for Harry's affection and settled into a comfortable place at his side. Their quest could be accomplished in full on the morrow.

The weak morning sun shone through narrow windows upon Margaret at her prie-dieu. Her rosary slipping silently through her fingers, she offered up her prayers without the benefit of her elaborate chapel with its candles, relics, and jeweled crucifix. Soon,

Harry would be ready to wake and Margaret would have their heavenly help already gathered around them.

This thought gave her hope when they made their way to the Herbert London house. Lady Anne continued to care for Henry as she had before her husband's death, but the boy was too old to be in the primary care of women. Margaret planned to petition George of Clarence for custody with Harry taking over Henry's education.

She was uncertain how much advantage to expect with one York brother over the other, but opportunities had been few in the years since she had been briefly allowed to raise her own son. Margaret had to grasp the chance while she could.

Lady Herbert greeted Margaret as she would an old friend, and Margaret, for her part, smiled as though this woman's husband had not stolen the earldom of Pembroke from her brother-in-law, Jasper. It was easier to be sympathetic now that the man was dead.

False niceties made Margaret's skin crawl, but she had prepared herself to offer them. Anne was more than a decade older than Margaret and had borne a dozen more children. Rather than see this as a disadvantage, Margaret stiffened her posture to emphasize her slender build and expensive gown.

Anne could not but have noticed, but she had been born a Devereaux and had been raised to allow others to see only what she wished them to observe. She offered wine and sweetmeats with an air of complete nonchalance. Margaret would never know that Anne hated women like her who teased the eyes of husbands whose wives could never maintain a slender form while bearing them their quiver of sons.

Harry was oblivious to the women's inner turmoil of emotions as he greeted Anne and offered her praise for the decorum and accomplishments of her children. He made clear that Henry could not have been in better hands, unless they were those of his mother. He charmed them both and calmed their secret jealousies without even trying, smiling as he pushed copper hair from his forehead that immediately fell back to disarray.

Margaret felt more comfortable once the polite amount of time had passed allowing her to bring up the business they were all gathered there to discuss.

"I am thankful for the care you have provided for my son," Margaret began, "however, I am sure you can appreciate that I hope to have his wardship granted to my husband for him to complete Henry's training through these formative years."

Anne dipped her head politely, but offered neither encouragement nor refusal.

Again, Harry entered the conversation. Beginning with a quip from his own boyhood, he managed to bring Anne around to a discussion of what she might hope to receive were the wardship transferred. Margaret gazed at her husband, love and awe more evident on her features than she would have liked. Had she, even after all these years, underestimated him?

As Anne chuckled under his attention and pledged her willingness to cooperate with the necessary negotiations, Margaret realized that she had. Her prayers that evening would gladly include a confession of her own pride alongside her thankfulness for the husband that God had blessed her with.

Margaret shocked Harry with her eager affection after leaving the company of Anne Herbert. Uncertain what he had done to earn it, he happily received it. Only when Margaret turned her attention to the next day's agenda, did he begin to realize what he was being rewarded for.

Her only roadblock was George, Duke of Clarence.

"How shall we best approach Clarence?" Margaret asked, looking to him with greater respect than she often did. "You managed Anne to perfection," she admitted. "What do you recommend as our way forward with the duke?"

Margaret did not mind admitting that one of her failings involved reading other people and easing them to her point of view. It was enough that she recognized that Harry did have that power, and she could utilize it.

Harry cleared his throat and pulled uncomfortably at his doublet. What Margaret saw as plotted skill, he only knew as being himself, but he would offer what he could.

"His grace has always thought much of himself, as I suppose most of us do," Harry finally ventured. "Clarence enjoys praise and wine more than most – likes to see people in awe of his majesty," he finished with a shrug. He felt this was nothing that his wife did not already know.

Margaret frowned. She could only hope that the York prince had enough other concerns that the fate of one young boy did not worry him enough to waste time in lengthy negotiations. Composing herself, she prepared for the first, though it most certainly would not be the last, appointment with the man who hoped to be England's next Yorkist king.

December 1469

The Christmas preparations going on around Margaret could not lift her spirits. The wheel of fortune continued to turn, and she always seemed to find herself at the bottom. She knew her husband meant well with his advice, but it did not make the pill any easier to swallow.

Her efforts of the past six months were for naught and, in fact, might have put Henry further out of her reach than ever before. If God increases our faith through trials and tribulations, she thought, I will have a greater faith than anyone in England. She forced herself to listen as Harry carried on.

"The fact is that our negotiations with Clarence have put our loyalties into question," he said with a shrug. "It may have seemed logical to plea with him for custody while he and Warwick had Edward in hand, but now that they are at peace . . ." he did not finish, only shrugged again.

That was the way of things, Margaret knew. All her life, loyalties and alliances had been everchanging. Now that Edward was reconciled with his cousin and brother, it was she who was under suspicion rather than the men who had fought against him. Her hands clenched in anger at the unjustness of it.

She had lost her son again. Clarence no longer had the power to hand him over to her, and the king would not consider it.

Harry reached out and took her hands, gently forcing them open so that he could caress them with his own. His lips compressed worriedly, evincing his frustration. Margaret was a more than capable wife and loving in her own way. He wished that there was more he could do for her than offer the reasoning behind her latest disappointment.

Margaret looked into his sky-blue eyes, so beautifully surrounded by his russet hair, and sighed. She knew that he would do more were it in his power. He had befriended Edward and his sycophants to the best of his ability on her behalf. Their efforts just had not been enough.

"I am sorry, Harry," she said, squeezing his hands in return. "I should have been more patient." She shook her head at herself, knowing it had been her own actions much more than her husband's that had caused this. She blew out a frustrated breath and admitted, "I knew that it would be better to wait. Knew that Warwick's power was not assured."

Harry placed a hand on her cheek, halting her words and worried quaking. "You are a mother who loves her son," he said with an endearing smile. "What tender woman would not have done the same in your place?" Giving her cheek a final pat, he leaned back in his seat and added, "Besides, you had my full support. I cannot blame you for a sin that is just as much my own, more so because it is my duty to guide you."

Margaret offered him a small smile that did not reach her eyes. He was such a comfort to her. For a moment, she wondered, not for the first time, why God did not bless her with a child of his. Would another child reduce her hunger to hold her first? She did not know.

"His ways are not our ways," she whispered, and Harry nodded in grim agreement, as if he knew exactly what she had been contemplating.

~ ~ ~ ~

The Yule log burned, and Margaret felt that angry fumes from her own mind were swirling in the air with the festive smoke. Garlands of greenery and the scent of roasting meat could not cheer her as she strode purposefully through the hall in search of her husband.

Once she located him, she demanded without preamble, "Will he truly marry his daughter to Edouard?"

With a gesture, Harry dismissed his chamberlain, with whom he had been discussing the needs of the household to comfortably stave off the cold winter months. He turned to his wife without frustration, exuding a calm that was often a balm to her fiery moods. Ignoring her tapping foot and raised eyebrows, he considered her inquiry thoughtfully rather than provide the response that she would have preferred to hear.

"I am not sure," he slowly replied to give himself more time to think. "On one hand," he stated, holding one hand out as though it held his words, "Edward might see marrying his daughter to the Lancastrian heir as a certain way to bring peace. On the other," his other hand joined the first in a see-saw motion that demonstrated the immeasurable weight of the options, "that would leave any sons he may sire vulnerable to rebellion in their sister's name."

Margaret huffed. She had already worked this out for herself. The king's offer of Elizabeth of York as a bride for Margaret of Anjou's son seemed to be a card he was playing rather than a legitimate offer. "It would make more sense if he did not have hope of having more children," she observed from the point of view of one who would know.

Nodding, Harry agreed, "Yes, reuniting the York and Lancaster lines would be in his interest if his only hope fell to his daughters. However, Elizabeth Woodville has proven she is a good breeder, if nothing else."

This truth made Margaret's brow furrow. The queen produced one child after another while Margaret's womb remained empty. Yet, it was an ache she had long grown accustomed to. Her thoughts must be for the future, but what would Harry think of her latest idea?

"She would be an ideal wife for Henry," she stated, forcing her voice to remain casual.

Harry's eyes widened at the idea only for a fraction of a second before he became thoughtful. With a shrug, he admitted, "It is not a bad idea, if only Edward could be convinced."

His tone did not carry much hope. Why would the king waste his daughter's hand upon a boy few had reason to recall existed? "She is likely to go to neither," Harry gently pointed out. "A prince of Europe is a more likely match for Princess Elizabeth than any Lancastrian."

The lines of Margaret's face deepened as she considered this. Of course, it was true. She could strategize all day long, but only the king had the power to give Henry the golden future she envisioned for him. She glared at Harry as if it were all his fault before storming away.

The chapel brought Margaret some peace and helped her release her anger. She prayed for God to increase her trust in his plan. Only when her thin form began to tremble with the cold did she move to stand. She stared at the crucifix as she stood before the altar, not wishing to leave the chapel and take up her duties just yet. Would that God saw fit to reveal just a glimmer of his plan to her!

A soft clearing of a throat broke her reverie and caused her to turn toward its source. Harry leaned casually against the doorframe, watching her with love in his eyes. Suddenly flooded with remorse, Margaret ran to him. She buried her head in his chest and realized that she took this man too much for granted. When she looked up at him, he offered her a wide grin.

"Oh, Harry," she sighed. "I am such a harridan at times. How do you bear with me?"

Fine lines formed at his eyes, and he appeared slightly confused. "That is not the way I see you at all, dear Margaret," he said.

Margaret felt her heart flood with love for this man who

stood by her and wanted everything that she wanted, if only to please her. He smiled again, seeing her face brighten. As he lowered his lips toward hers, Margaret realized that God had revealed a bit of his plan, if not the portion that Margaret had been searching for. He may not have given Margaret her son, for now, but he had given her Harry, and that was no small gift.

~ ~ ~ ~

The Advent fast was broken with gusto by most of Harry and Margaret's household. The four weeks of limited diet and increased prayer in preparation for Christmas was more of a challenge to most than it was to Margaret. She enjoyed the feeling of devoting herself body, mind, and soul to God – an empty stomach but heart full of the Spirit.

Still, she smiled when she observed the joy evident on rosy faces as mince pies and savory soups were happily devoured. Even Margaret sighed with pleasure as she let sweet almond cream melt on her tongue. Her fasting would not be replaced with gluttony, but she welcomed the return of a few of her favorite dishes.

Harry had been reuniting with his beloved honey mead and now stood and gestured for the tables to be cleared away as if he could sit still no longer.

"Where are those musicians?" he loudly inquired, and everyone laughed as servants scurried to transform the hall from a dining area to a dance floor.

For a few hours, Margaret allowed herself to forget about the Earl of Warwick and King Edward. She even set aside her concerns for Henry, just for a little while. He was cared for well enough, and Margaret had to trust that God was with him when she could not be. Twirling across the floor in the strong arms of her husband, Margaret laughed and let the joy of the season into her heart.

Harry's eyes glowed with pleasure and the inhibition that the honey mead lent him. With a flush covering her cheeks, Margaret smiled when he pulled her closer to him. How thankful she was that this one person in the world knew her inner heart and understood that there was so much more to her than a cold exterior. She knew that people believed that, as a second son, he had married her for her name and fortune. Few would have believed the genuine connection between them. It was what kept her from despair.

Laughing breathlessly, she laid a hand on Harry's chest. Other dancers prepared for the next tune, but she needed to rest. "I am not accustomed to dancing all night," she admitted, longing to remain in his arms.

Harry's rust-colored hair was disheveled and his face glowing with energy, yet he bowed to his wife and led her to one of the chairs lining the walls of the hall. He briefly left her there, and Margaret watched his progression through the room to acquire beverages for them. His finely tailored doublet did more than speak to the riches required to obtain it. Margaret did not often have lustful thoughts, for they led to the painful reminder that she was barren. However, as she watched her husband and the ladies' eyes that followed him, she felt a warm satisfaction that he was hers.

Returning with cups of spiced apple ale in hand, Harry sat near enough to Margaret that she felt the heat of his body along her left side. She closed her eyes and sipped her ale, reveling in the moment, for she knew, as much as she enjoyed it, that she would not soon give herself such freedom to be frivolous again. These moments were to be treasured but not too often repeated or they could lead to a life of idleness and vice.

"Shall we retire, my love?" Harry's deep voice came to her in a soft whisper with his breath warm upon her ear. She felt her body tingle in anticipation.

"Surely, you are enjoying the dancing," she argued, though she was not certain why she did so. She wanted him to take her to bed, but could not help pointing out that he seemed to be enjoying himself already.

He took her hand in his and leaned in close. "I have danced enough for tonight," he said, all lighthearted joviality gone from his face. His eyes bore into her as if they were the only ones in the hall, and she could only nod her acquiescence so great was the lump that formed in her throat.

Harry stood, pulling Margaret with him. He did not announce that they were retiring, knowing that the attention would make Margaret uncomfortable. All would be taken care of in their absence, so they quietly slipped from the hall.

March 1470

Margaret could have been a statue as she stood overseeing the preparations in the courtyard. She did not move and could barely breathe knowing that Harry would soon be leaving to join the king's forces against those of Warwick.

The peace established at Christmastime had been short-lived indeed. If Warwick had been disillusioned with Edward before, he was furious now that lands and titles had been taken from both he and his brother to further enrich the king's more faithful followers.

The move had somewhat surprised Margaret. Little as she liked Edward, few could deny his aptitude for leadership. He had succeeded where his father had failed in grasping for England's throne, but now he seemed to be going out of his way to enrage the man who had been his greatest aide in that achievement.

These thoughts ran through Margaret's mind while men checked saddlebags and smacked squires into action. She seemed to be the only person not in motion. Harry stepped in front of her, and still she did not even move her eyes to meet his. She stared blankly forward, straining to see what the future would bring.

"Margaret," Harry said, lowering his face to force her gaze to meet his.

She finally blinked, and her focus locked onto the bright azure eyes before her. Her lips pursed into a thin line, and Harry knew her too well to expect an emotional farewell in front of his men. Margaret tried to keep anger from overtaking her and prayed for God to bless Harry even if that meant continued success for the York king.

"Return to me," she quietly ordered her husband.

She did not reach for him and would not shed a tear where anyone could see it fall, but she saw in his eyes that he understood her love and need for him. Harry tipped his head to her in acceptance of her command.

"With God's blessing, I will," he replied.

He would have embraced her, she knew, had it been up to him. Public displays of affection would not have bothered him, but he was always kind enough to cater to her preferences. As he turned and left her without another word, she wondered if she would mind if he made an exception now and then.

Margaret maintained her position until her husband's retinue was out of sight and she could no longer hear the pounding of hooves upon the still frozen ground. The cold permeated her limbs and the breeze pulled hair from her hood, but she felt as if moving from that spot gave events permission to proceed. Without knowing where fortune's wheel would stop, she was afraid to let it turn.

A soft voice interrupted her thoughts, and Margaret jumped.

"My apologies, my lady," said Margaret's chief lady-in-waiting as she curtseyed low before her. "You are like to catch a chill if you remain in the cold much longer," she pointed out without raising her eyes to Margaret's.

Recovering her composure, Margaret nodded and mumbled a response. She realized when she took her first step toward the warm rooms awaiting her that her toes had gone numb. Struggling to keep her pace precise and not stumble in frozen clumsiness, she strode inside with the woman hurrying in her wake.

Her comfort could come later. Margaret's first destination was the chapel. God's aid to her husband and his troops was much more vital now than Margaret's warmth. As she knelt in order to beg God to watch over him, she wondered about Henry. No longer in the guardianship of a man who would be called to fight, would he remain safe at Pembroke? She prayed for him as well, just in case.

Time passed, and Margaret had no idea how much before she said her amen and stood. Her limbs were numb and stiff, but she felt satisfied that she had done what she could. The rest was in

24

God's hands. He had not made her a man who could bear a sword in battle. He had chosen to make her a woman who fought in the much more dangerous spiritual realm.

Margaret was frequently found in prayer throughout the days following Harry's departure. She would never express her doubts or concerns to anyone, but she worried that Edward would question Harry's loyalty. When Harry immediately obeyed the summons, would he be welcomed back into the fold or be under continued scrutiny as Warwick had been?

She thanked God that Harry was so charismatic. It was a trait that he shared with his king, and Margaret prayed that it made reconciliation between them swift and complete. Of course, if the upcoming battle went to Warwick, their long efforts to gain the trust of Edward IV would come to nothing....again.

All she could do was wait and pray.

~ ~ ~ ~

Thankfully, she was not forced to wait long. Within a fortnight, a messenger arrived, and Margaret immediately recognized her husband's livery beneath the dirt and grime. Her breath caught in her throat, but, as thoroughly as she searched for it, she did not observe any signal of bad tidings in his appearance. A sigh of relief escaped her, but no one noticed. Everyone's attention was drawn to the new arrival who would carry news of so many of their loved ones.

Margaret did not allow herself to be part of the welcoming pandemonium. Her dignity meant more to her than instant gratification, so she waited calmly for the messenger to be properly presented to her. He quickly was, as was his duty, so Margaret had not sacrificed much. She nodded to him as he bowed, her face giving away not an iota of the concern and fear that would not completely dissipate until he spoke the words she needed to hear.

"I am sent to you with the news of our victories in the field," he began.

Deep brown eyes searched her for a reaction but found none. Her hands remained clasped in her lap atop her soft velvet skirts, and her face was unreadable. Margaret knew better than to release her emotions until she had the entire story. Was Harry injured? What about the king? Had they suffered losses that would be detrimental to his long-term success? Margaret did not celebrate the victory of battles that came at the expense of the war.

Seeing he should continue, the messenger forged ahead, "Sir Henry Stafford has come through the battle unharmed, as has his grace, King Edward."

"Praise God," Margaret whispered while lifting a single small hand to indicate that he should continue.

He was warming to his subject, despite Margaret's lack of encouragement. "We may have had fewer men than the rebels," he said with a satisfied grin, "but ours were the greater quality. In short order, they were retreating so quickly that their kits were abandoned in pieces strewn throughout the field."

By the faraway look in his eyes, Margaret could perceive that he was watching the events play out again, but she had little patience for his wandering thoughts.

"And Warwick?" she demanded.

Shaking his head and bringing his attention back to the woman before him, the messenger smiled more broadly. "He is in exile, my lady. Running like the devious fox that he is from the forces of our great King Edward. And Clarence with him."

"Clarence?" Margaret whispered. The king's brother defied him once again. How many times could he be forgiven?

"They have made for Calais but will be disappointed by their welcome there," the man continued while raking a hand through grimy hair, making it stand on end.

"What do you mean?" Margaret asked, leaning forward in

eagerness despite herself. "Warwick is well respected in Calais. He held that captaincy for the king not long ago."

"That he did," the messenger agreed with a nod in appreciation of Margaret's intellect, "but King Edward has sent messengers ahead of Warwick's party. They will be denied, and the great Earl of Warwick will find himself with nowhere to lay his head but the block."

Margaret leaned away from him and loudly cleared her throat. She did not make habits of underestimating her enemies or assuming their defeat. "And Clarence went with him?"

"Aye, my lady, and with the Lady Isobel great with child."

Margaret's eyes widened at this news. Richard Neville might take risks for himself, but he must be running scared indeed if he brought along his daughter at such a time. Isobel had been married to the king's brother of Clarence in one of Warwick's many plays for power that had yet to pay off.

"They will have nowhere to go," Margaret stated, beginning to feel the messenger's optimism infect her. She needed to think about what it all would mean for her. For Henry. "Take your refreshment in the hall," she said, gesturing for the man to leave her. "I may speak to you more after I have given thanks for our king's victory."

He bowed his head toward her, disappointed but not entirely surprised that this great lady did not inquire after more details. He would obtain greater reward from those gathered in the hall who were waiting eagerly to hear his tale. He mumbled his thanks and left her alone with her thoughts.

Unfortunately, Margaret's thoughts could not lead her to a place where she was reunited with her son. Harry was safe, but Edward was, once again, victorious. Would she ever see Henry again?

September 1470

The defeat and exile of the once powerful earl of Warwick forced Margaret to reconsider additional efforts at peacemaking with the king. If Edward IV was the one with power to restore Henry to her household and the titles that should be his, then it was Edward to whom she would humble herself.

Yet, she knew she must take care. Overflowing with charisma himself, Edward easily recognized posturing on the part of others. She must persuade herself of her loyalty to him before she would ever be able to convince him. Reconciliation with the crafty York king would be difficult, but it was not a challenge Margaret shied away from.

Throughout the summer months, as news slowly leaked to her of Warwick's trials in France, Margaret weighed her options. Jasper, her former brother-in-law, was also in France. Should she await his next move, knowing he would act in his nephew's best interests? Would Warwick return? She cared little for the fate of most men, but was terrified that she would make the wrong move on Henry's behalf.

Henry remained in the Herbert household, making it possible for Margaret to send him the occasional missive and package of items he might find useful, but she longed to see him. She wondered how he felt, a boy almost a man who had so long been separated from his mother that it might simply seem the way of things from his point of view.

It was moments like this that Margaret found comfort in only two things: Harry and her faith. Her strength was stretched to its limit in order to trust God with the future she could not see, and it was only Harry's presence at her side that bolstered her with the support she needed. After a few moments in the chapel, she went in search for her husband.

Harry should have been overseeing the harvest or analyzing

the household accounts, but Margaret knew that she would find him with his horses. He could afford to be frivolous thanks to his wife's good management of their estates, and she loved to see him filled with joy as he was when he acquired a fine new courser or led his destrier into a joust. She found him in close comradery with a stable boy, his doublet loose and sleeves shoved up.

Margaret smiled fondly, not at all concerned with the mess Harry was making of his good hose. The laundress would have her work cut out for her, but Harry's happiness was worth that and much more. Enjoying these moments before her husband noticed her presence, Margaret drank in the sight of him, strong and handsome and hers.

"John, you must pardon me for a moment," Harry apologized to the boy unnecessarily when the reflection of sunlight on Margaret's gown caught his eye. "I have news that my good wife will be anxious to hear."

Her smile falling as an eyebrow raised in question, Margaret wordlessly took Harry's offered arm and allowed him to lead her to a nearby bench. She examined his features for clues of his news, but Harry's countenance rarely gave a grim report. Once they were seated, he took her hands and gave her a lopsided grin.

"God has heard your prayers, Margaret," he said, squeezing her fingers.

She waited for him to elaborate, but he seemed to feel that he had already imparted his news. Margaret nodded eagerly to indicate that he should carry on.

"Oh, of course," he said with a shake of his head that sent bits of straw flying from his russet locks. "Warwick has returned."

Margaret leaned back, worried that she might topple to the ground otherwise. "But what does it mean?" she asked herself as much as her husband.

"Edward has been forced to flee!" Harry announced.

Margaret's eyes widened in disbelief. "You must tell me all," she demanded. "Start at the beginning."

If Harry felt that he was being treated like a child, he did not express any dismay. Instead, he obediently retold of the miracles that had unfolded. Following Warwick's humiliation and failure of the spring, he was back in force. "Even the king underestimated him," Harry cried with another shake of his head. "He was unprepared to face Warwick, so he was left with no choice but to run with little besides his coat and brother of Gloucester with him."

"Run? Run where?"

Harry shrugged. "They found a ship willing to take them on, but where the brothers of York will reappear is anyone's guess. Warwick makes his way to London."

"To free King Henry from the Tower!" Margaret cried, finally catching Harry's enthusiasm. "Edward has truly been defeated?"

As she said it, she felt an odd feeling of disappointment. After all these years, would the news of Lancastrian victory simply be a story her husband told her sitting upon a garden bench? Should it not feel as if the earth had moved and the world was celebrating? The horse Harry had been examining stomped a hoof and breathed heavily as if informing Margaret that was the best she could hope for, but she drew her eyes back to Harry and found him waiting for her to say more.

"We must go to London!" she announced. Margaret was already beginning to stand, but Harry held her hands firm.

"Caution must yet be employed," he reminded her, taking the unusual position of the more prudent one. "Edward does not likely count himself down and out."

"It does not matter," she objected, pulling her hands free of his and standing over him. "We will be in London to see the rightful king reinstated, and Henry shall be at my side."

Margaret rushed away without awaiting Harry's response.

31

There was much to do, for she would have her son at the center of the Lancastrian celebrations. She would not allow another king to brush him aside. Of course, this one would not. Henry was his namesake and nephew.

They would deal with retribution from Edward should it ever come. Today, Margaret prepared to take her rightful place at the court of King Henry VI.

October 1470

If the power of Margaret's will could conjure a person, Henry and Jasper would have long ago appeared. She had not left the window of the London house since finishing her morning prayers. Jasper, brother of her late husband, Edmund, had come from France in Warwick's wake and had retrieved Henry from Pembroke, which had once been his, as he traversed Wales gathering troops. They would be in London for the presentation of the rightful king, Jasper's half-brother and Henry's uncle.

Margaret smoothed her dress, though not a wrinkle or mislaid fold was present. Then her hands moved to her hair and finally fidgeted with her jewelry. Her wait had been too long, but it was these last hours that strained her most. Each person who came into view caused her heart to leap before it settled back into her chest in disappointment.

Would Henry be taller than her now? He must be, she thought. He was thirteen now, and Margaret was a diminutive woman. Would his hair have darkened the way many children's did as they grew into adulthood? She could not help but worry how well his memories of her matched up with her memories of him.

And then they were there.

She recognized Jasper first, but did not allow herself to dwell upon the fact that her own child appeared to be a stranger. The young man at her brother-in-law's side carried himself with her own reserve and dignity, eyes taking in everything while his countenance gave up little. Margaret smiled at the similarities while also frowning a bit at the thought that others saw her that way. Then, she shook herself from stillness and ran to greet them.

Before she got too close, Margaret slowed her pace and allowed the rhythm of her breath to become steady. Everything within her longed to lunge toward her son and gather him in her embrace, yet she stood firm as Henry approached and knelt before her to receive her blessing. Margaret solemnly gave it, memorizing the feel of his skin beneath her fingertips as she traced the sign of the cross upon his forehead. When he stood, she looked up at him several inches above her and gave in to her desire to hold him.

She felt him stiffen for just an instant as her arms wrapped around him, but he quickly yielded to her affection and loosely enveloped her in his own arms. Her head upon his chest, Margaret closed her eyes in order to etch the moment into her memory. Even with Henry VI returned to his throne, Margaret would take nothing for granted and would assume nothing of the future. If this was the last time she held her child, she would fix a perfectly formed remembrance of the experience in her mind.

Too soon, Jasper cleared his throat and the moment was gone. Henry took a step backward as he was released, and Margaret's hands resumed their task of unnecessary smoothing and tidying. It took a moment for her ingrained manners to remind her to greet her brother-in-law as well, but the wide grin across his face told her that he understood. She smiled in return as her eyes more fully took in his appearance.

Jasper might have been more easily recognized from a distance, but now Margaret could see that he had been no more spared from aging than Henry had. Where her son was fast becoming a man, Jasper's hair had gone grey at the temples and a starburst of lines led away from his eyes as he smiled at her. It made her wonder how she appeared to him, though she was more than ten years his junior.

He bowed, as if demonstrating to Henry what was proper, before straightening and pulling Margaret into a rough embrace.

"It's been too long, Maggie," he said, making his beard scratch against her cheek.

"That it has, brother," she replied, grinning at his use of her old nickname. It made her feel like she was Henry's age again.

"Praise God that you are both here and King Henry is also once again in his rightful place."

"Amen," Jasper agreed in a booming voice. Few had more reason to be thankful for his half-brother's return to power than he did.

Turning to direct the men inside, Margaret observed, "We have much to discuss, but I am sure that you would first like to freshen up from your travels and fill your empty bellies. Let me show you to your rooms where everything you require has been laid out."

With murmurs of assent, they followed her and expressed their pleasure at having their needs foreseen. Not wishing to leave their presence so soon after finally seeing them again, Margaret forced herself to make her way to the kitchen and supervise dinner preparations while Jasper and Henry settled in. She hoped that they would be staying for a very long time.

When they rejoined each other for the evening meal, Margaret quickly realized that Henry was in awe of his Tudor uncle. He could not have remembered him well from his childhood. However, he had grown up hearing of Jasper's exploits, making him appear more than mortal man to his young nephew. That was fine with Margaret. She wished for Henry to look up to Jasper as one of the closest things he had to a father. Though she had married Harry while Henry was still young, the connection with Jasper was different, and Margaret saw much of her Henry's father, Edmund, in him.

Jasper was loud and jovial, telling stories that were likely embellished for Henry's sake, emphasizing the glory of victories while remaining silent on the hardships of exile, hunger, and loss of position. Margaret said little, content to observe and enjoy their companionship. Only when she felt herself growing too weary to remain at table much longer did Margaret interrupt the tales that

Jasper likely could have woven all night.

"What have you heard of the king?" she was anxious to know. "I believe we should present Henry to him as soon as possible."

Jasper nodded with his forehead crinkled in thought. "I agree," he said before turning to Henry. "He will restore both of us to our rightful positions, my boy."

When he slapped Henry on the shoulder in the universal sign of brotherhood, Margaret winced at the force of it but Henry grinned as though he had earned a rite of passage.

"The day after tomorrow then," Margaret said as she pushed away from the table and stood. "You will have tomorrow to rest, and then we will present ourselves to the king."

The men nodded to Margaret as they clinked their goblets together in agreement.

"It is settled then," Margaret said. A scarcely perceptible gesture brought servants to clear the table, though Jasper and Henry held their goblets away from their helpful hands. "I am off to the chapel before I am at risk of falling asleep while at prayer. Good night to you both."

As she left the room, Margaret paused behind Henry's chair. Her hand moved toward his auburn locks, and she considered placing a kiss on the crown of his head. But no, she decided. He was too old for a mother's coddling as much as his mother may desire it. She forced her hand to take up her rosary beads instead and strode toward the chapel.

~ ~ ~ ~

Henry's fine green doublet belied his true age, and Margaret was proud of the young man she would present to the king that day. In his own dark red velvet, Jasper also was striking to look upon. My handsome Tudor men, Margaret thought to herself with the pleasant feeling that her heart might burst.

She felt an arm slip around her waist, and leaned toward her husband without needing to turn to be certain that it was him. Harry squeezed her close to his side, sharing in her joy and anticipation for what the future now held for them. If either held any doubts about the strength of Henry VI to rule, they only had to look toward his son, Edouard, a strapping young man who would ably take up the crown when the time came.

Prince Edouard was only a few years older than Henry, and Margaret envisioned them becoming close in the newly established Lancastrian court. But she was getting ahead of herself. Margaret shook her head and freed herself from Harry's grip and her imaginings. The future, bright as it may be, must wait. Today, they would see the king.

Warwick had freed King Henry from the Tower but moved him only as far as Westminster. Here the frail man, who appeared aged well beyond his true years, was accepting the obeisance of faithful Lancastrians and Yorkists who felt it was their best option to do so. The sight caused Margaret's optimism to fade, though she would not let anyone know her inner concerns.

Warwick had attempted to wrap the king in the trappings of royalty, but Henry appeared weighed down by the velvet and ermine, his head bowed beneath the gold crown. How could he carry the weight of a country on his shoulders if the cloak that Edward made appear light was too much for him?

These thoughts coursed through Margaret's mind as they awaited their turn to be presented to King Henry in Westminster's Great Hall. Her efforts to distract herself from her concerns by examining the soaring ceiling with its huge wooden beams were fruitless. Each time her gaze found the king, her heart sank a little. As she dared to meet the eyes of others in the crowd, Margaret saw her own worries mirrored. She forced herself to straighten her spine and exude confidence, if not in this man then in his son who would soon join them from his exile in France.

Margaret's thoughts kept her from noticing the passing of time, and she soon found herself face to face with the king. She curtseyed low with Harry and Henry on either side of her. Jasper, a half step behind, protectively kept close to Henry's other side. A light touch from a thin hand covered loosely with papery skin told Margaret to rise.

King Henry's gaze was vacant with glimmers of awareness attempting to break through. Margaret found herself saying a silent prayer for Prince Edouard's safe and quick arrival. The man in front of her would be no match for Richard Neville of Warwick, not to mention the swarm of Yorkists who did not yet consider themselves to be defeated.

"Brother!" As soon as the formal greeting was complete, the king embraced Jasper with fervor.

"Henry," Jasper replied with a slap to the back of his king that made Margaret cringe and thank God that the older man was not knocked down, "it has been too long. Far too long."

"Indeed," Henry agreed before turning his eyes to Margaret. "Little Margaret," he said with a grandfatherly grin.

"Your grace," Margaret replied with another curtsey, her eyes downturned. As she began to rise and reach toward her son to present him, she saw a peculiar look cross the king's face. He seemed confused or lost in time when his eyes turned to young Henry. Before Margaret could speak, the king rose his hands toward her boy and spoke with great authority.

"This truly is the one whom both we and our adversaries must yield."

Margaret's mouth went dry, though she knew not how she would respond were she able, and the king had not finished.

"He will rule over this great dominion as is his right."

She willed her eyes to move from the strangely focused stare of the king. How she desired to see how Henry was reacting or look to Harry for guidance, but she could not avert her gaze. Did the king mistake her son for his own? What did he mean by this strange and wonderful prophecy?

Then King Henry's face cleared and he once again turned to Margaret.

"And how is this husband of yours?" he asked, patting her hand before grasping weakly at Harry's.

Margaret barely heard Harry reply that he was well and make inane small talk with the king because she was looking at her son. He too looked as though he were trying to decipher the meaning behind his uncle's unexpected revelation. His mouth moved to speak, but a quick shake of his mother's head silenced him.

Harry's hand was at the small of her back. "We cannot monopolize the king's attention," he said with a smile of regret toward Henry and an understanding look in his eyes toward her.

"Of course," Margaret agreed, recovering herself she began to back away.

"Do come and visit me often," the king almost begged in a childlike voice. "I do appreciate a friendly countenance."

"We shall, your grace, and are greatly honored."

With that, the highly anticipated meeting was over, but Margaret had more questions and concerns flying around her mind than ever before.

"What could he have meant by it?" she demanded of Harry as soon as they were alone that evening.

"I am quite sure that I know no more than he does," Harry replied with a shrug.

"What is that supposed to mean?"

He could only shrug again. "You know as well as I do, Meg, that the king never fully recovered from his catatonic episode. It was clear that he knew not who he was addressing."

Margaret was surprised to feel her spirit shrivel a bit at his observation. Did she truly believe it had been a prophecy? But how? And did she really want it to be?

Harry's arms went around her. "Meg, you are working yourself into a worry over nothing. As much as I give him my support as king, old Hal does not reside in the same world as you and I."

Nodding, Margaret quickly buried her head in Harry's chest to hide the disappointment she was certain he would be able to read upon her features.

"There," he soothed, rubbing her back. "All will be well. Young Henry will be restored, and you will enjoy the time with him that has been stolen from you thus far."

Finally, Margaret spared him a smile. "You are right. That is all that truly matters, that we are able to be together as a family as we never have before."

Leaving Jasper with his royal half-brother, Margaret was happy to take custody of her son and treat him to a visit to her favorite estate at Woking. The party did not speak much while on the road, since Margaret rode in the comfort of her carriage while Henry preferred to be on horseback. Margaret used the time to plan the week ahead. She was determined that it be a time that would provide them both with memories to treasure for a lifetime.

Harry divided his time between Margaret's carriage and the back of his courser. Margaret could see that he enjoyed Henry's company but could no longer stay in the saddle for countless hours as he could in his youth. Compassion swelled in her chest for this man who always put the desires of others before his own. When he sat next to her, he gave no indication that it was not his first choice.

She rewarded him with an affectionate smile and patted his knee. "What shall I tell the cooks to prepare while Henry is with us?" she asked him as she came to the realization that she did not know what her own son's favorite dishes were.

Harry grinned and a hand went to his belly as though he could imagine the banquet he would soon enjoy. "Ah, let us have a fine lamb," he did not hesitate to request. "Oh, and a spice cake. All growing boys love a good cake."

"I shall see that it is done," she assured him. If Henry could not have his favorites, Harry would.

"He is bound to enjoy anything that is edible," Harry said, once again reading into her doubts and worries, "as do all boys his age."

"Thank you, my love."

Margaret would not let this precious time be consumed with worries. She moved nearer to her husband and closed her eyes to enjoy the closeness of him.

Some of the reserve seemed to have left Henry by the time they arrived. Margaret knew she owed that to Harry and his easy-going manner. Everyone warmed to him, and her son was no exception. As she directed her staff on where items should go and what she wanted unpacked, Margaret observed their familiar banter and prayed that she, too, would gain access to Henry's well guarded soul.

The rooms appropriated for Henry's use were sumptuous and facing east to make the most of the morning sun. Margaret had selected these in favor of a view of the courtyard and hoped that she had chosen well. Instead, Henry could look out over Margaret's neatly trimmed orchard and see the deer park beyond. Surely, he would also wish to hunt while he was there.

As the time to retire to bed approached, Margaret joined Henry before the cheerful fire in his sitting room. Warm light flickered around the room, welcoming Margaret in to find a cozy chair. As she entered, she held out the book in her hands.

"I thought you might find this to your liking," she said,

nodding for Henry to take it from her. "It is a copy of Jehan Froissart's chronicles."

"Thank you, mother," Henry said with interest as he eagerly took the proffered manuscript. He shared her love of books and they were frequently part of the care packages she sent to him.

Margaret was content to sit before the fire and watch while Henry carefully turned a few pages. After a moment, he closed it as if the temptation to begin reading were too overwhelming to ignore if he left it open.

"I shall enjoy it," he assured her, turning his attention back to her.

"And what else should you like to do during your stay?" she asked. "I can organize a hunt if you like. Harry might already be doing so," she added with a knowing grin.

"That would be quite agreeable," Henry said, returning her smile. Just the mention of Harry's name seemed to put him at greater ease.

Margaret chose companionable silence for a few moments before putting her next inquiry to him.

"Have you been kept well, Henry?"

She examined his face as he considered his response. He appeared somewhat surprised, as if he had not considered that he might not be treated well by his guardians.

"I have," he finally decided.

Margaret took a deep breath and slowly released it. She could not complain if her son had inherited her own habit of keeping inner thoughts closely guarded. He seemed content enough. That would have to suffice. She stood and smoothed her skirts before taking a step closer to him.

"I shall give you my blessing for a good night then, and you may perhaps enjoy the chronicles for a bit before finding your bed."

Henry remained seated so that it was easier for his mother

to reach down and make the sign of the cross upon his forehead. She indulged her desire to place a kiss there as well before making her way to her own comfortable bed.

The next day, Harry eagerly took up the plan for a hunt while Margaret gave Henry a tour of the estate, taking mental notes along the way of issues that she would later discuss with her chamberlain. Henry was satisfactorily impressed with the grand moat and elaborate gardens, to say nothing of the palatial manor itself that wrapped around a fine courtyard.

As they strolled through the orchard, Henry touching the early fruits that were within his reach, he asked her, "What do you think the king meant?"

Margaret was uncertain how to respond, so she pretended to be investigating a branch that might need pruning. What had King Henry meant by his strange prophetic words, and what could she say about them that could not be construed as treason?

"Might that he was simply confused?" she said, unconvincingly.

Henry shrugged, but she could see that he was still contemplating the words as would any boy told that he would become king of England.

She was glad when he said no more on the topic, for she was afraid of where her own thoughts took her as well.

Instead of thinking forward to a future that could not possibly be, Margaret decided to tell her son about her first visit to the royal court.

"I was not quite ten years old when mother allowed me to attend the St George's Day festivities at Windsor alongside her. I felt so grown up and honored," Margaret recalled with a soft smile. "The castle appeared to my younger self as a vision out of a dream," Margaret said, gazing into the sky, "especially when the knights of the Order of the Garter made their solemn procession into St

George's Chapel for worship."

She glanced at Henry to see if the tale captivated his interest, and he politely nodded for her to continue.

"Yet the most memorable image of that special time was meeting the queen. I was fascinated to learn that this exotically beautiful young woman shared my name."

"As the king shares mine," Henry said, his grin as wide as his mother's.

"Just so," Margaret agreed as they continued strolling through the fruit trees and her memories came to life in her mind. How she had admired the lovely young queen and her pious husband. Young Margaret could not have foreseen how terribly wrong everything would turn.

Remembering Margaret of Anjou forced Margaret to consider present difficulties. It was only thanks to the courage and implacability of his queen that Henry found himself on England's throne again. Margaret wondered to herself if she could ever find such strength within herself if God demanded it of her.

King Henry, not an impressive figure when Margaret had first met him in 1453, was even less prepossessing now that he was frail, aged, and weakened by his mental lapses. Surely, Margaret knew other men who had reached fifty years of age without it wearing down on them quite so thoroughly as they seemed to have the poor Lancastrian king.

Suddenly, Margaret realized that her son was speaking and she forced herself to release the meanderings of her mind for another time.

"My apologies, Henry," she said with chagrin, "my mind was wandering. Can you repeat that?"

Thankfully, his inquiry related to the trees within the orchard rather than their own confusing family tree that threatened – or promised – to place her son curiously close to the throne.

November 1470

It seemed that no time at all passed before they were preparing to leave Woking. Jasper had previously been granted Henry's wardship, and, as much as Margaret hated to turn him over to anyone, she took comfort that it was her beloved brother-in-law who would be responsible for his care. Logically, she knew that Henry would need to learn how to be a man of the court and would not likely remain in her household even if they had enjoyed a normal family situation, but her heart still fractured at the thought of his leaving.

Instead of contemplating Henry's absence, Margaret occupied herself with compiling the gifts that she would send with him when he left. Books, clothes, blankets, and a dagger were included in the trunk she prepared him. Jasper was a practical man, so Margaret knew better than to send Henry off with too many luxuries. And at the back of her mind was the fear that the Lancastrian king could not hold the throne for long with Edward of York planning his revenge.

Henry would need to be flexible and mobile. He would need to know how to live as a soldier, for his future was far from certain.

Margaret tried to make the most of the journey that would take her son from her, but, before she knew it, Jasper was greeting her and she was attempting to match his joy at seeing her. She loved Jasper, but his presence meant that her time with her precious son was at an end.

"Margaret, I see time with our Henry has done you well," Jasper exclaimed when he saw her.

Though he meant it as a compliment, Margaret could not help but wonder how world weary she must normally appear for a week with her son to do such wonders. Jasper did not seem to listen to her mumbled response anyhow.

"Henry has recalled all loyal Lancastrians back to court," he continued with a grin splitting his face. "Red roses are returning home from exile."

She managed a smile while thinking that she only cared about the Lancastrian rose she was sending away, but Jasper was right. The rightful king of England was restored to his throne. She should be giving thanks to God and considering how Henry could serve his uncle in a few short years.

Over dinner, Jasper's joviality eventually got the best of her. His joy and faith in his half-brother was contagious, and the future looked bright.

If Margaret must send Henry away, she was glad that it was Jasper who would take responsibility for him. Besides Harry, there was no one on Earth she trusted more. She could not halt her mind from traveling back in time to one of the scariest points in her life when Jasper had cared for her, still a child herself with a babe growing within her. Her husband, Edmund, was dead before having the opportunity to meet his son.

Those days had left her terrified. Already fearing facing childbirth when she had so recently played with dolls, Margaret had received news of Edmund Tudor's death. She had been so certain that he was the husband God had intended for her, but at that moment she could not help but wonder if she – or God – had made a mistake. Would her child survive? Would she?

The war, which was at that time between King Henry and the Duke of York, Edward IV's father, had only recently begun to rage, but now it defined her entire life. Had it not been for Jasper during that time, Margaret would not have been able to lift herself from her pit of despair. Henry had been born healthy, and she and Jasper had quickly decided that Harry Stafford would make an advantageous husband for Margaret. God still had a plan for her after all.

The memory forced Margaret to look at Henry in a new light.

She had been a young mother and widow at his age and must stop thinking of him as a child. Her desire to claim him and keep him young would not serve him well. Margaret resolved at that moment to think of Henry as the young man that he was and see that his future included the types of honors that his king foresaw for him.

December 1470

The next month brought Christmas festivities, which Margaret aimed to make as cheerful as possible despite Henry's absence. Harry's health gave her increasing concern and caused her to spend extended time at prayer on his behalf. Whatever heartache she had encountered, she could not imagine how she would cope with anything without Harry at her side.

"Oh, Meg," Harry sighed, attempting to keep the pain from his voice, "you are too good to me."

Margaret kept the grimace from her face. After all, if Harry was man enough to pretend that his joints did not scream in agony with each movement, she could certainly control her own reaction. The sores on his skin bothered him surprisingly less than the stiffness in his bones, but the oozing ulcers threatened to raise Margaret's bile. At least until she glimpsed his face. Seeing his courage and reluctance to make her privy to the true extent of his pain left her with nothing but compassion for his condition.

"My love," she whispered as she rubbed soothing oil into his fingers, "it is you who have always been far too good to me." He began to object, but she cut him off. "I know that some mock me for my coldness and that I have failed to give you a son, but you have never caused me to feel that I have disappointed you."

He lifted his hand to her chin and forced her to gaze into his eyes. "Because you never have," he insisted. "Margaret, my love for you will last an eternity."

She kissed him quickly to mask the tears in her eyes. An eternity, yes, but how much longer on this earth?

January 1471

Margaret refused to wallow in sadness. He may not be in the strapping health of his youth, but Harry was still very much with her. Their wedding anniversary celebration this year would be more elaborate than ever.

Since they were first married, they had enjoyed inviting their friends and family to share in their anniversary with feasting, dancing, and entertainment. Margaret found that it was a wonderful way to chase away the dreariness of winter. With so much warmth and laughter inside, who could spare a thought for the bleak landscape outside?

Planning the annual party seemed to be an effective medicine for Harry as well. He moved with the energy of a younger man as he assisted Margaret in preparing Woking for more than one hundred guests.

A luxuriously warm velvet cloak was ordered from London, and Margaret felt giddy as a young girl when she presented it to her husband. The firelight reflected on the rippling fabric as Harry pulled the cloak from its packaging, and Margaret's heart swelled as Harry admired her gift.

"I will look finer than the king in this!" he exclaimed, wrapping it about his broad shoulders.

Margaret stepped forward to arrange the fall of the fabric and caress its fine texture. "You always look finer than the king," she said and placed a light kiss on his cheek.

"Our guests will wonder where our windfall has come from," he joked. "I hope you have also had a fine dress made for yourself."

"Of course, I have," she assured him. "I could not appear before our party in rags now could I?" She ignored Harry's raised eyebrow as he wondered what clothes she owned that could be considered rags. "I shall wear tawny and some velvet to match your own."

"Ah, we shall be king and queen of our own domain!" Harry cried in joy as he pulled Margaret into his arms. "I can think of no greater moment to celebrate than the day that God gave you to me as my bride."

Margaret happily returned his embrace. "You are my bright light in this dark world," she said, molding her body against his.

"We will not talk about darkness," he insisted. "Our home will be filled with those we love, and we shall give thanks to God for our many blessings."

"Amen."

~ ~ ~ ~

The party was just as Harry had predicted. Margaret was filled with joy as she watched young people dance and exchange meaningful glances. The feasting was more than equal to the recent Christmas festivities that had been celebrated. Harry continued to be less burdened by his joints and even joined in a few of the dances, pulling Margaret onto the floor with him.

Servants in Stafford livery always seemed to be close at hand to offer a beverage or sweetmeat. Music flowed out of the hall late into the night, and feasting left everyone full and content. At the head table, after several hours of celebrations and in front of a happy audience, Harry stood to address his guests.

"My beloved wife and I wish to express our thanks to you all," he began, holding up a goblet as if to toast each one of them. "You have traveled through some harsh weather to join us as we celebrate thirteen years of wedded bliss."

He was forced to pause as raucous cheers rose and goblets clinked together. Margaret was touched by the sentiment but also felt a blush rising to her face. Harry soon made to speak again, and the crowd fell quiet to listen.

"God gives us each blessings and trials," he continued more somberly. "Each of us has lost loved ones in these turbulent times that we live in, but we have also gained friendships and loved ones that might not have been joined to us otherwise."

Nodding and grumbled agreement met his words. How would their lives be different if Richard of York had never challenged Henry VI's right to the throne?

"I choose today to be thankful for the great gifts that God has bestowed upon me, as little as I deserve them," Harry said, raising his voice and his glass. "And the most generous of his gifts has been my dear wife, Margaret."

Harry drank deeply from his goblet and the crowd cheered and followed suit. Margaret smiled and gazed at him through the tears in her eyes. "And I praise God for you, husband," she whispered though none could hear.

Margaret hated to see their guests depart, but she could see that the days of festivities had left Harry worn and weary. She would treasure the memories of these days for the rest of her life, however long God gave them.

March 1471

Margaret scarcely had time to convince herself that the Lancastrian restoration was real before it was threatened again. Rumors of Edward of York's invasion plan came to her through her cousin, Edmund Beaufort.

As soon as his entourage filed into her courtyard, she knew why he was there. The air around Woking felt heavier with their presence. She wished that she could order them to leave. If only that would make his message less true.

Her cousin sat atop his destrier as if he had been born there. No one who gazed upon the well-built young soldier would question that royal blood ran through his veins. To their great dismay, even the Yorkists had a difficult time denying it. Their hatred for the Beauforts ran deep and cold.

Margaret knew why Edmund was here, but her feelings were torn regarding his objective. He bantered with his men as they filed in and dismounted, acting for all the world as if they would not soon be riding to their deaths.

Could she bear to send Harry with them?

Uncertain whether to proclaim that his health made Harry's participation impossible or urge him to join the Lancastrian army, which was in need of every good man it could get, Margaret decided that she would leave it completely up to Harry. Without feeling the Holy Spirit urging her toward the correct path, she was fearful of steering him wrong.

Margaret felt Harry's presence at her side, and her worries naturally calmed. Gazing into his eyes, she knew that it mattered not what his desires were, he would not be physically capable of joining Edmund. His conflicting emotions were as clear on his face as hers must be.

She took his hand and forced a smile to curve her lips. "Let us greet my cousin, dear one."

Margaret was surprised when Harry pulled her to him instead of following her forward. Then she noticed how heavily he was leaning upon his cane. He preferred that people outside their household not see him use it, so the fact that he made no secret of his need for it now alerted Margaret to how severe his current pain was.

"Oh, Harry," she sighed, laying a small hand on his stubbled cheek. "Go and make yourself comfortable. I will bring Edmund to you that he may make his case for the glories of war."

Harry did not respond, only bowed shallowly to her with an ironic grin before shuffling painfully away. Could it have been only months ago that he swept her off her feet to dance? Margaret was still watching him and concentrating on keeping tears from her eyes when she heard Edmund's voice behind her.

"Cousin Margaret!" he bellowed. They may have shared Beaufort blood, but Edmund enjoyed being the center of attention in a way that Margaret never would. He entered a room wanting every eye to fall to him and every ear to listen eagerly to the wisdom he would impart.

"Edmund," she greeted him simply as she turned and curtseyed to him. He would not gain his desires here, so she would at least salve his ego with courtesy. "You are looking very well. Please join Harry and I in the solar while your men find their refreshment in the hall."

"My thanks to you," he said. Gesturing to his second in command to see to the men, Edmund followed Margaret inside.

"I have news about Edward of York," he began before they were seated.

"Of course, you do," Margaret countered. "Why else would you be here with men-at-arms?"

If Edmund was at all taken aback, he did not show it. Instead he turned his efforts to Harry whose frailties were not evident when he was sitting comfortably in his cushioned chair.

"Stafford, the Yorkist demon gathers troops in Flanders. We must be prepared to repel him when he makes his inevitable attempt to reclaim England."

He leaned forward, speaking with passion and urgency that made Margaret wish Harry could go with him. Until she imagined him dying on the field. No, God had a better plan in mind for her husband.

Harry was already shaking his head. "Would that I was able, Edmund, but I have suddenly become an old man." He shrugged and smacked his aching knees in dismay. "I would not admit this to many men, but I am afraid I would not be capable of mounting my horse."

Margaret frowned, upset that Harry felt the need to unman himself to avoid his duty. Edmund, however, was brushing the objection aside as if he had hardly heard it.

"Nonsense," he insisted. "Once you are in the field, you will feel ten years younger. It is this life of leisure that saps your strength." Seeing the flush rise to Margaret's face, Edmund tried to jokingly add, "Margaret spoils you far too much."

With a half-hearted laugh, Harry said, "If only that were the source of my complaint, as good as my Meg is to me. It is a much more serious ailment than laziness that has cursed me." He shrugged and turned to Margaret as though he could add nothing more.

Before Margaret could confirm his diagnosis, Edmund spoke again. This time, a hint of anger crept into his lighthearted tone. "Is it your loyalty to Buckingham? Surely, your duty to your king outweighs that to your family."

"Edmund!" Margaret objected. "Harry has never failed to demonstrate his loyalty to our good King Henry. In fact, we were just with him in London, as you surely know."

Taking a deep breath to calm himself, Edmund rubbed his face with his hands before running them through his disheveled hair. Suddenly, Margaret realized how weary, how desperate, he was beneath his confident veneer.

"My apologies to both of you," he relented. "Is your health so bad as that, Harry?" he asked more sincerely.

Harry nodded reluctantly. "I am afraid it is."

"Then I shall pray for your healing. You are too valuable of an ally to not have at my side," Edmund said as he stood.

Margaret smiled at him. She knew that Harry was not a leader of men or an irreplaceable soldier, so she appreciated that Edmund would at least make him feel as though he might be.

"And I shall pray for your success and for the well-being of our king," she said as she followed him to the hall to gather his men. Neither of them commented on the fact that Harry remained seated, only mumbling words of farewell to Edmund's retreating form.

April 1471

The following month, Margaret had reason to wish she had pitied him less and pressed Harry more to join Edmund and his Lancastrian forces.

"How can you do this?" she demanded. Angry tears formed in her eyes, only serving to increase her fury.

"Margaret," Harry said through teeth that were clenched in his efforts to mount his horse through the pain that raged through his joints. "I have to join our king. I love you and am devoted to your son, but King Henry has as little chance of claiming victory over Edward as I have of returning to the health of my youth." Finally settled as comfortably as possible in his saddle, he concluded, "I will ride with him."

"Think of the men you fight against," she insisted, grabbing his bridle to keep his horse in place. "Edmund, Jasper....what if Henry is there?" The very thought made her stomach twist forcefully.

"Jasper knows better than to bring Henry to a fight likely to end in a rout, and Edmund is his own man. He knew what he was doing when he took up arms against the Yorkist army. Maybe it is his desire to die gloriously, but it has never been mine."

Margaret did not know whether to be thankful or furious that her husband could look at war so objectively. Instead of being torn between his Stafford, York, or Lancastrian loyalties, he simply determined with clarity which side was going to win. Even if Margaret could bring herself to agree that the Lancastrian cause was lost, she would not admit it.

"Henry is our anointed king. You cannot ride against him."

Harry pulled the bridle gently but firmly from her grasp. "I can, Meg, and I will. For your sake and your son's," he said quietly. "Forgive me, my love, but it appears that God is a Yorkist."

His men fell in line as Harry turned his horse away from her and toward London. He turned back just long enough to request, "Please pray for me. If it is God's will, as it is mine, I will return to you with all speed."

And then he was gone, and Margaret was left not knowing whether to curse him or beg God to protect him.

~ ~ ~ ~

By the time word reached Margaret that Edward had easily marched into London and been reproclaimed as king, she had already completely forgiven her husband and only prayed that he was not in too much pain and that his ailments would not make him vulnerable on the field. King Henry or King Edward - it mattered little if she did not have Harry.

Waiting for news brought back memories of ten years earlier when she was a young mother desperately longing for news of Jasper and Harry when rumors of Towton began trickling in. A horrid, bloody battle by all accounts, Margaret had been afraid that both of her protectors would be lost fighting for Henry VI against Edward of York.

That time, her waiting and praying had been rewarded with Harry returning home unharmed, though part of a defeated army. Could God plan the same result today? It would be everything Margaret desired to have Harry home and Edward defeated.

She could only pray that Jasper had been as wise as her husband in deciding when and where to fight. Yet, let him be cleverer about it than her cousin, Henry Beaufort, had been. He had changed his coat one too many times, and fell to the executioner's axe several years earlier. It was one of the many incidents that caused such a desire for revenge in Edmund Beaufort. He would never support Edward. Margaret could not help but think of Henry Beaufort from time to time since Woking had been his before his death. It was a rare sign of favor toward her that Edward had granted the estate to Margaret.

Where was her son, she wondered, as the battle-ready York king prepared to face-off with his own cousin, the Earl of Warwick? As Margaret waited for news, her knees grew sore and bruised as a result of her time in the chapel.

Could she possibly pray for the lives of every person she cared about to be spared? It seemed too much to ask, even of God. But who would she find herself mourning? One of her brothers-in-law, King Henry or Jasper? Even worse, Harry or Henry? She could scarcely bear to contemplate the possibilities.

Early reports served only to confuse and frustrate her. Due to fog and mismanaged troops, the Battle of Barnet was a mystery to those waiting for information regarding loved ones. Determining who had fallen and who had simply been separated from their men was a challenge during and in the aftermath of fighting. Margaret sent men daily to bring her news, knowing that eventually the truth would be revealed.

A fortnight after Harry had left and when Margaret's nerves were thoroughly frazzled, word finally reached her that Warwick had been killed in battle. She would not mourn for this York cousin who had belatedly switched sides to serve his own interests. Far better men than he had been lost in these battles between cousins. But word of Warwick's fate came to her with news of her husband that chilled her to the bone.

Harry had been wounded and was being sent home. The messenger had been sent ahead so that she could prepare to make him comfortable and see to his needs. Margaret swallowed the bile that rose in her throat and nodded to the young man who had given her the news for she could not form a single word. She turned from him and went to prepare her husband's death bed.

And it was not even over. Although Warwick was defeated and King Henry once again imprisoned, Margaret of Anjou was reported to be on her way from France with the valiant Prince

Eduoard ready to lead his own troops in defense of his father. Would Jasper, with Henry in tow, join him?

May 1471

Harry was brought home and put to bed. His wounds were not as severe as Margaret had feared. However, combined with his already failing health, they threatened to overtake him. Margaret trusted the running of the household to her chamberlain and dedicated her time to prayer and caring for Harry.

She continued to send men out for news, though she found herself less concerned than she should have been for the fate of the Lancastrian queen when she landed in the west. It was her son she was desperate for news of. She would prostrate herself at the feet of Edward IV if it meant that Henry would be safe.

A breathless messenger brought her information that was just incomplete enough to leave her wishing she knew nothing at all.

"The armies are expected to clash near Tewkesbury," he said in a rush. "The queen has tried to outrun Edward of York and give her allies time to reach her, but he pushes his men like a hound from hell....pardon, my lady."

He lowered his head as his cheeks flamed, but Margaret paid no attention. Was Jasper one of the men struggling to reach his queen and prince in time to die alongside them, or had he decided, as Harry had, that the York warrior could not be beat?

"Edward and his brother, Richard of Gloucester, strive to cut them off before they can escape into Wales," he continued when Margaret failed to remark upon his obscenity. Margaret noted that he could not hide his respect for the York brothers though he had always proven a loyal member of her household.

"And my son?" she reminded him of his true purpose, but he was shaking his head.

"Jasper Tudor is not believed to be with the queen's troops, but he may join them before battle is met," he said with a shrug.

Margaret shook her head in frustration. Why could not one

of these informants bring her the news she needed to hear? Where was her son? Waving the man away, she took a few moments to rub her temples and calm herself before making her way to Harry's room.

For him, she made the news sound brighter. "There is no word of Jasper and Henry within the queen's camp. Jasper has likely taken Henry back to Brittany."

"He is an intelligent man and is dedicated to Henry's protection. You may trust him to do what is best for him," Harry agreed, and Margaret was surprised to find that she did feel somewhat better.

Harry was swaddled in blankets despite the increasing heat that promised a steamy summer. But he seemed comfortable, so Margaret was content. She went through her routine of tending his wounds, rubbing oil into his joints, and treating his abscesses and found it almost soothing. Instead of reminding her of his poor health, it made her feel as though she was doing something with purpose. He bore it all with a loving smile, even when she knew the treatments must pain him as much as the injuries.

"I am sorry, Margaret," he said after her ministrations were complete.

"For what?" Margaret asked, her eyebrows raised in wonder of what wrong he could have perpetrated while exiled to his bed.

"Had I not gone to Edward when you asked me not to, I would not be here. You would not be caring for a dying man who earned his wounds in the service of a king you do not believe in."

She was immediately at his side with his hand clutched tightly in her own. "Don't do this," she ordered. "Do not apologize for doing what was right. Do not talk about dying. Just let me love you."

Tears streamed down her face as she started rechecking bandages and wraps that she had just put in place, but Harry stopped her frantic motion and pulled her to him. He said nothing more, for he could not take back what he knew to be true, but he held her and they pretended that everything would be alright.

~ ~ ~ ~

"The king and prince are dead."

Margaret stood in the doorway to Harry's room and made the announcement quietly enough that he could almost convince himself she had not said it.

"I am so sorry, Meg," he said, raising his arms to beckon her into them.

She walked slowly across the room, crawled onto his bed, and burrowed into his chest as if she were a child longing for the comfort of a father. "It is over," she whispered.

"What happened?"

She lifted her face from the bedcovers and gazed up at him. "Tewkesbury. Too few had time to come to the queen's aid, and her son was butchered. Of course, she lost all heart after that. My cousin, Edmund, is also lost."

"But the king?" Harry asked in confusion. "He was in the Tower."

"Yes, he was," Margaret agreed, her voice hardening. "He has allegedly died of melancholy at hearing the news of his only beloved son." She narrowed her eyes at her husband, daring him to defend the murder of the simple, devout man who had been their king.

"Edward is a warrior, but he is also a king. Now there will be peace," Harry pointed out.

"Because there is nobody left to fight!" Margaret cried, jumping from the bed, too full of anger to be still. "He has massacred anyone who might claim his throne."

Harry patted the bed to call her back. When she turned from him in refusal, he said, "He has done no different than Margaret of Anjou has attempted. Your King Henry was not a soldier in a time

65

when a warrior king was what he needed to be. I am sorry, Meg."

She had gone to the window, though she was not really looking outside. Margaret's head drooped and she wondered how the bright future that had been promised could have been so thoroughly destroyed. "Henry had been returned to his throne for less than a year. Now all is lost," she said.

"Not all," Harry quickly corrected her. "Is there word of your son?"

Margaret only shook her head. She did not believe that he had been at Tewkesbury, but she also did not know where Jasper had taken him. Was he safe?

June 1471

Still uncertain about Henry's whereabouts and safety, Margaret learned that she was not the only one looking for him. Edward, now unchallenged king of England, had sent Robert Vaughn to find and arrest the Tudor men. From that moment, every one of her men who went out carried with them messages that instructed Jasper to immediately take Henry into exile.

She would lose no one else to this undefeatable York king. Henry was young. He could bide his time.

Margaret's days were consumed with caring for Harry. She had moved beyond praying for his recovery to wondering if it would not be more merciful for God to take him home.

In constant agony from his wounds, open sores, and swollen joints, Harry appeared to be an old man. He could no longer rise from his bed, and he, never a vain man, had requested that none besides Margaret and his physician see his reduced state. The only way she could bear to see him like this was because she knew the alternative and that she would have to cope with it soon enough.

She took cold comfort from the fact that she did not believe God would take both her son and her husband from her.

September 1471

Margaret and Harry had both grown drawn and thin, he from his deteriorating health and she from constant worry. Clean and rebandage the wounds that refused to heal. Dab salve onto an ever increasing number of leprous lesions. Massage oil into joints that could not be soothed. The routine continued to calm but no longer comforted Margaret.

It broke her heart to see her handsome, lively husband reduced to this husk of his former self. When the sores reached his face, he asked Margaret to keep the doctor away.

"There is nothing he can do for me at any rate, Meg," Harry admitted ruefully. "If my long-suffering wife must see me like this, at least no one else need be exposed to it."

Margaret conceded to his wishes, knowing he was right and not wishing to cause him unnecessary humiliation. Despite the enemy that slowly ate away at him, she could see the man she had fallen in love with every time he smiled in his efforts to raise her spirits.

"How I love you," she sighed as she attempted to apply salve gently enough to not cause him additional pain.

"And how could you not? I being such a handsome devil," he said with a wink.

She laughed, but quickly covered her mouth with a hand. "Oh, Harry. I am sorry," she cried, horrified that she had found humor in his condition.

"Why would you be?" he asked. "I am also devastatingly amusing."

Margaret smiled and lowered her hand. Despite it all, he managed to be sweet old Harry sometimes. He did it for her, of course, but also for himself. Stuck in bed for months, who would not want to remember that they had once been so much more?

Other times he would be serious. One day he had begged her

to bring in a nurse. He seemed terrified that Margaret would share his fate.

"My dear husband," she had calmly replied, "if the leprosy were going to claim me, it would have done so before now. God protects me in his goodness that I serve as a dutiful wife to you."

His objections had slowly died away as he accepted the logic of her argument. Afterwards, Margaret had wondered if he had been embarrassed for her to watch his continuing decline so she increased her efforts to demonstrate that she loved him as much as she ever had.

In truth, she missed his arms around her and the intimacy of their bed, and she was sure that he must as well. Sometimes, she would lay by his side, but they had mostly been reduced to holding hands. The most touch they shared was when she tended to his wounds.

When her thoughts were not consumed with Harry, she was overtaken with concern for Henry. It had been some small consolation when Robert Vaughn, the man Edward had sent to capture the Tudor men, had instead been captured and beheaded by Jasper. Margaret knew that they had been forced to flee into exile after that blatantly illegal act, but she had heard nothing since. Weeks of waiting were rubbing her nerves raw.

Margaret's quick stride had been reduced to a slow shuffle as she made her way from Harry's room to the chapel. She found she had little reason to hurry anywhere anymore.

Lowering to her knees, she felt pain shoot through the bruises that were already there and knew that they would grow darker by the morrow. She was angry at herself for even noticing such a minor injury when compared to what her husband lived with. She shifted, grinding her knees into the hard floor in punishment.

Her prayers were filled with Henry and Jasper. There was no

longer a Lancastrian cause to pray for but she could not bring herself to pray for the York king, so her efforts were focused on these two men. Keep them safe and the rest of the world can fall apart, she thought. It already had anyway.

After several moments, Margaret had the sensation that she was no longer alone. Ending her prayers somewhat abruptly, she rose to discover who would disturb her at such a time. With a word of admonishment on her lips, she turned, but before she uttered a sound a smile split her face.

The grubby, road-weary messenger grinned back at her.

"They are in Brittany, my lady. They are as safe as two coneys in their burrow."

Margaret felt faint, so she moved to grasp the back of a nearby pew. Henry was safe, and God had saved him for a purpose. She was suddenly just as certain that he would soon take her husband. She nodded, making the messenger wonder what she was thinking. God's bargain was accepted, Harry's life for Henry's. She would see to it that her son reached his full potential.

October 1471

When Margaret shared her ambitions for her son with Harry, she was surprised by his reaction.

"For the time being," he said with greater energy than she thought he was capable of, "you must demonstrate loyalty to our king."

He did not need to say King Edward. There was only one king of England now. Margaret bowed her head in submission. Much as she might hate the thought of it, she knew that Harry was right. Especially if she was to be left without his protection.

"I will, Harry," she reassured him. "Edward will have no reason to doubt my motives. Maybe he will even allow Henry to return to England and serve him."

Harry had either extinguished his stores of energy or did not wish to express doubt in Margaret's hopes because he did not comment further upon Henry's future.

"Give our king no reason to doubt you and marry someone who has served him well."

Margaret was astonished. "Harry! How could you speak of such a thing?"

"Because I must," he insisted. He would have grabbed her hand, but his strength had reduced him to opening his fingers in the hope that she would notice and willingly take them up. She did. "I will not be here for you much longer, and you will need someone who can protect you and Henry."

"But I love you!" Margaret cried, not wanting to envision herself with another man.

"I know you do, but it may be some time before we are reunited. You will do what you must."

Tears squeezed between her lashes as much as she attempted to screw her eyes shut, but she knew that he was right. She would do what was necessary, if not for her sake for Henry's.

Margaret did not have vivid memories of her childhood before her marriage to Edmund Tudor, but she did remember the terror her mother expressed upon the vigilante execution of William de la Pole, Duke of Suffolk. That moment ingrained in her the truth that anyone could die for treason, and one must always be certain that their king had no reason to doubt them.

"I will," she promised Harry. Edward would have no reason to question her or her son. To her horror, eligible partners began to come to mind, but she quickly forced them away.

The next morning, Margaret found Harry lying peacefully in his bed. He was no longer in pain and the sores that had appeared raging red upon his skin the day before seemed pale and faded. He looked years younger now that he had entered eternal life.

Margaret kissed him for the last time before carefully washing his body and preparing it for burial. Her tears would come later. She had a bargain with God to uphold. Once Harry was lovingly dressed in his graveclothes, Margaret went to her own room and undressed.

The hair shirt felt rough against her skin, and even more so when she layered her underdress and gown over it. With each move, she felt her skin becoming raw. It made her smile to know that she would finally understand some small portion of what Harry had gone through.

Her knees were permanently bruised, but now when she entered the chapel she prostrated herself fully on the unforgiving stone floor. The autumn chill seeped into her bones, and she was glad again to suffer in service to her God and memory to her beloved. When she rose painfully an hour later, she looked at the crucifix but spoke to Harry.

"I will see Henry raised up. I will make you proud. I love you, Harry, and will see you again soon."

Epilogue – July 1483

Margaret's face could have been carved from stone as she lifted the train of Anne Neville's heavy coronation robes. She had never trusted Richard of Gloucester, and now everyone would see him for the devil that he was. Now that it was too late. The procession made its way into Westminster Abbey where Richard and Anne would be jointly crowned as king and queen of England.

Margaret could not believe that after more than ten years of serving King Edward and marrying a man who had never been accused of Lancastrian sympathies, she was left with this. Edward had finally been prepared to forgive her son and allow him to come home, if England could truly be considered Henry's home when most of his life had been spent in exile.

The pardon for Henry Tudor lie unsigned among King Edward's papers when he suddenly died just weeks shy of his forty-first birthday.

Instead of seeing the astonishing ceremony taking place in front of her, Margaret's mind brought up the vision of the crumpled missive that had brought her the unwelcome news. She had thrown it into the fire, the flames reflecting in her eyes as her heart hardened against the world that seemed firmly set against her. She remembered screaming, as she wished she could do now. The dogs had set to whimpering in their kennel and the horses had shifted uneasily in their stable as the sound of rage and heartbreak echoed through the darkness of night.

Still staring into the fire, Margaret had made a vow that night, though she knew not if she made it with God or the devil when she promised, "I will see my son in his proper place. I will do anything to see him return to England in glory."

Her resolve to see it done had only increased in the three months since Edward's death. Richard had claimed the throne for himself, claiming his brother's sons were bastards. Suddenly, the battles of the last three decades seemed nothing but a prelude. This was where Margaret's real battle would begin, and she would see to it that the crown was removed from Richard's head if it was the last thing she did.

After all, she still had her son, and Elizabeth Woodville, Edward's displaced queen, still had a passel of beautiful daughters who each carried royal Plantagenet blood.

It was time for Henry to come home.

Afterword

Margaret married Thomas Stanley less than a year after the death of Henry Stafford. Their marriage was more of a business agreement than a romance, an arrangement that seems to have suited them both. This gamble did eventually pay off for Margaret when the actions, or lack thereof, on the parts of the Stanley brothers led to the defeat of Richard III at Bosworth Field.

Margaret finally saw her son returned to England in August 1485, as its king. The story of Henry Tudor and Elizabeth of York continues in *Plantagenet Princess, Tudor Queen*.

Additional Reading

For those interested in reading more about the historical figures featured in this novel, I recommend the following sources:

Margaret Beaufort: Mother of the Tudor Dynasty by Elizabeth Norton

Winter King: Henry Tudor and the Dawn of Tudor England by Thomas Penn

Margaret is also a secondary character in the first novel of my Plantagenet Embers trilogy, *Plantagenet Princess, Tudor Queen: The Story of Elizabeth of York*.

Author's Note

Margaret Beaufort is an intriguing historical figure. She was both pious and calculating, a combination that was admired in a 15th century man but which continues to fuel disagreement when found in a woman. I myself have accused poor Margaret of worse acts than I believe she is actually guilty of in *Plantagenet Princess, Tudor Queen*. Somehow, even without meaning to, my Margaret turned into the villain that so many accuse her of being.

It is a fine line to walk for the historical novelist to decide what personality to assign to famous people. Determining how to portray Margaret Beaufort is something like deciding what to do with Richard III. Regardless of the final product, someone will be disappointed. Just as many people were upset that I made Margaret 'bad' as those who were just as concerned that I had made Richard too 'good'. In truth, I think they were both human.

With this novella, I hope that I have redeemed both myself and Margaret somewhat. I do believe that everything Margaret did was driven by an ambition to see her son raised up. While she probably did not always have a crown in mind for him, she certainly would have snatched the opportunity when it presented itself. Having two sons myself, I understand what that powerful love might motivate one to do in their interests.

Much less is known of Margaret's husband, Henry Stafford, whom I have called Harry in an effort to reduce confusion. He received unknown wounds in the Battle of Barnet and may have suffered from leprosy, an illness that can affect the joints and cause abscesses. He died in October 1471 of unknown causes that may have included some combination of these ailments. Henry and Margaret did hold a celebration of their anniversary each January, which I interpreted as evidence that this marriage was a love match for Margaret in a way that her other marriages never were.

After Henry Stafford's death, Margaret devoted herself to her son's cause, gaining herself a reputation for being a formidable woman who may deserve as much credit for the birth of the Tudor dynasty as goes to Henry Tudor himself. Whether one loves her or hates her, it cannot be denied that Margaret Beaufort was a woman who fiercely loved her son.

Samantha Wilcoxson

Once a Queen
A Story of Elizabeth Woodville

Samantha Wilcoxson

To all who have been forced to make impossible choices.

June 1483

"You still have your children to think about. Even if we are all bastards."

Those parting words cut Elizabeth to her core. More than a fair share of anger had been directed toward her in her life, but this wound was deep because it was her own daughter who had inflicted it. Did Bess think that she did not care, that she would not do everything in her greatly diminished power to set things aright?

Her world had fallen apart just as much as her daughter's had when Edward died.

Elizabeth's eyes took in the hastily packed trunks and scattered belongings that were all that remained of her time as queen of England. She had ensnared the heart of a king, but this was all that was left of that life. Treasure beyond anything she could have imagined as a girl had enriched her entire family when she married Edward, but she had never considered what might happen if he were not there to stand between her and her enemies.

When Elizabeth left this dark sanctuary over ten years ago, she had never imagined that she might reenter it. That Edward might die. That their marriage might be declared invalid. That her children would go from being heirs to the crown to misbegotten bastards. Edward would not stride into Westminster Abbey to save her this time.

Normally, her hands would itch for something to do. She despised idleness, but as reality crashed down around her, Elizabeth sat immobile, staring into the dark void that was her new future.

Bess found her like that hours later, but she only noted the passing of time by the gloom and cold of the room and the stiffness in her joints.

"Mother, what are you doing?" Bess asked, her earlier anger dispelled by concern. "You will catch a chill."

Her words stopped short in realization of what she had just

said.

"Oh, mama, I'm so sorry," Bess said as she knelt before her mother, pools of her azure gown spilled around her. "How very thoughtless of me."

Elizabeth almost smiled as she patted the girl's copper head. Only Bess could turn her fury off so completely and quickly. Instead of continuing to revile her mother over her reduced status, she apologized for bringing up the painful subject of the king's passing.

As Bess continued to murmur soothing apologies, Elizabeth's mind brought forward the image of her dead husband. How could that glorious man, a soldier to make any man's blood run cold were they to face him across a field, die so young after taking ill with a minor chill? Edward had been a giant of a man, physically intimidating and able to fill a room with his personality.

Elizabeth was sure that God was playing games with her, but she had to shove the thought aside as she attempted to make sense of the apologetic babbling of the young woman at her feet.

"Bess, stop. For heaven's sake," Elizabeth demanded, taking her hands from her daughter's head in frustration.

Bess sniffled but ceased her words, and for that Elizabeth gave thanks. She could not bear another moment of it. Whether Bess was fuming with righteous anger or crying in sorrow, the very sight of her filled Elizabeth with undeniable feelings of guilt.

On her knees, with her golden-bronze hair spilling around her, Bess was the vision of an angel. Instead of giving her mother joy, it annoyed her. She knew that her eldest daughter was more beloved than herself without vivid reminders of how well-deserved that was.

"I am fine. Leave me," Elizabeth demanded, turning from Bess so she would not have to witness the hurt marring her perfect features.

Elizabeth refused to meet her daughter's searching eyes and

kept her countenance frozen until the girl left once again. Then she released a sigh, and bit her lip. Taking in the forlorn contents of the chamber, she wondered how she would save her family from this turn of fortune's wheel.

A restless night did not bring Elizabeth any closer to the answers she sought. She had grown so accustomed to Edward solving her problems and standing firmly between his family and the world. People accused her of scheming, but she had done nothing more than suggest to Edward what he might do. If recent events proved nothing else, they demonstrated that she had no power of her own.

Elizabeth picked aimlessly at her luxuriant bedcovers that seemed out of place within the abbot's lodging. She wondered at the time, then sighed. It did not matter. Nothing did. The sounds of her children's voices floated to her from outside the room, but it was not enough. She rolled over and closed her eyes.

When they next opened, Bess' concerned face filled Elizabeth's vision. She groaned, "What do you want?"

"Mama," Bess whispered, and it reminded Elizabeth of how she had spoken to Edward as he lay on his death bed.

"Stop it," Elizabeth snapped, throwing back the covers and shoving herself into a sitting position. "There is nothing wrong with me." If only that were true! Her hair was a tangled mass around her, and her eyes felt puffy and swollen as she glared at her eldest daughter.

Bess had backed away slightly in the face of her mother's anger, but she persevered. "I must apologize for upsetting you, mama," she said. "We have all been through so much. It was not fair of me to burden you further."

She gestured to a tray that she had placed near the bed. "Will you not eat, mama?"

Elizabeth glanced at the offering and was surprised to feel a stirring of hunger. Taking a bite felt somehow like giving up, so she turned her face away dismissively. "I am not hungry," she lied, not certain why she was being difficult or what she hoped to achieve.

"Very well," Bess accepted her mother's rejection demurely, annoying Elizabeth even more. "I shall leave it here for you to sample as it pleases you."

As Bess turned to leave, Elizabeth sharply felt that she did not want to be alone again. She would always be alone now that Edward was gone. Bess could not change that, so Elizabeth clamped her lips tightly over the words that she had almost released, begging her daughter to stay.

The next day, Bess returned leading a man who was easily recognized as a physician. The mysterious leather bag which held tools that looked as well suited to torture as healing gave him away. As Bess described her mother's melancholy to the doctor and thanked him for coming, Elizabeth lay silent, as though she were asleep with her eyes open.

Once the door closed to give the patient and physician privacy, Elizabeth was shocked into showing that she was aware of her surroundings. Her head snapped toward the physician's voice and her eyes widened in curiosity fringed with distrust.

"What did you say?" she demanded, though she had heard him perfectly well.

He bowed respectfully but did not repeat himself. Elizabeth had given him much information in those few seconds, and he saw that she was ripe for his plot. Instead, he riffled around in his bag for a bit to give her imagination time to run away with her. When she appeared to be growing impatient, he pulled a fine, narrow blade from the bag with a small cup.

"I am Doctor Caerleon. According to your daughter, your humors are in poor balance," he said, indicating that he would see her arm for bleeding.

Elizabeth bared her slender arm, but was not backing down. "Why would Margaret Beaufort send you?"

Her tone was commanding, but Lewis Caerleon was used to that. As she had said herself, he was in the pay of Margaret Beaufort, a woman able to make any man do her bidding with her regal voice and sharp eyes.

He busied himself with tying a fine cord around Elizabeth's arm and watching her veins bulge. "Ah, there we are," he murmured as he expertly sliced one open and held the cup to catch the streaming blood.

Elizabeth's eyes had not left his face. He appeared to be in his forties. Lines left his eyes and got lost in his greying hairline. His forehead creased from hours at study, but his mouth was soft without the fine lines that pursed increasingly around Elizabeth's own lips. She examined him boldly as he completed his tasks.

Caerleon did not speak again until his instruments had all been wiped clean and placed back into the dark bag that rarely left his side.

"I am here to serve the mutual interests of your family and my lady," he said as casually as if he were directing her proper diet.

Elizabeth narrowed her eyes, not realizing the aged, nearsighted appearance it gave her. "And what mutual interests could those be?"

Caerleon smiled, seeing that she was intrigued despite herself. His face was friendly, caring, not the face of an enemy's minion. This made Elizabeth trust him less.

His gaze moved around the room before finding its way back to the former queen. "What are your goals, your grace?"

Elizabeth met his eyes unashamedly for several seconds. Then she laughed loud and long, the sound sharp and displeasing even to her own ears. Suddenly quieting herself, she glared at him. "I no longer have any."

With a thoughtful frown, the doctor bobbed his head up and down, considering the sense of her words. "Maybe that can change," he said, standing and gathering his belongings.

Realizing that he meant to leave, Elizabeth held out a hand. "Wait! What do you mean? Why has Margaret sent you?"

He simply offered her his gentle smile and opened the door, making it impossible to continue without being overheard. Elizabeth fumed, but before she could think of any way to make Caerleon stay, Bess was in the doorway.

"Please see that your mother gets plenty of rest," he instructed Bess. "And do try to provide conversation and entertainment that might lift her spirits," Caerleon continued, allowing his gaze to stray back to Elizabeth. "She is sorely in need of some good news."

Bess had eagerly assented to the physician's orders, assuring him that all would be done to reverse her mother's decline into dark moods. She did not notice Elizabeth's gaping mouth and attempts to draw the him back into the room. With Caerleon gone, Bess returned to her mother's bedside.

"Now, let's see which of these foods tempts you," she said, retrieving the tray and placing it on the bed.

~ ~ ~ ~

Elizabeth remained in bed only to ensure that Doctor Caerleon would return, for, in truth, she was aching to put an end to her idleness. His words, as little information as they imparted, had been enough to stir her imagination and make her wonder what Margaret Beaufort could possibly want with her.

Margaret was one who was always about the edges of court. Her own semi-royal blood and advantageous marriages made her a woman of note, though she seemed to prefer to be alone. Only her first marriage had resulted in a child. Henry Tudor was the nephew of Henry VI, the addled king whom Edward had replaced and then murdered.

Several times over the course of Edward's reign, Margaret had held important positions and worked to gain favor within the Yorkist regime despite her Lancastrian roots. Elizabeth knew why, of course. Her son. Margaret cared for no one in this world besides the boy she could hardly know. He had been in exile for years. Edward had denied him permission to return to his mother, for there had never been an advantage in it for the king.

Elizabeth wondered. How could Henry help her?

She ran possibilities through her head, certain that hers and Margaret's minds worked in a similar fashion. Margaret would have known that a plot between them would need to be appealing on both sides just as well as Elizabeth did. What did Margaret know that she did not?

Scoffing at herself, Elizabeth had to admit that there could indeed be much that she did not know. The walls of sanctuary protected those inside from news of the outside world as well as from their enemies.

Sounds from just beyond her chamber door yanked her from her thoughts, and she had to force her face to go slack and her eyes to droop. Inanimate upon the bed, she hid her true energy as the doctor was admitted to the room. She thought she would explode as she remained motionless while Bess made small talk and explained that her mother seemed much the same despite her efforts.

As soon as Bess was gone, Elizabeth sat up on the bed, her eyes glowing with intensity.

"What message have you from Margaret?"

With a doubtful frown and questioning gaze, the Caerleon moved to the bedside and opened his bag. Elizabeth wanted to shake him.

"I am not quite sure what you mean," he said quietly as he

felt Elizabeth's face and peered into her eyes and ears.

Drained of what little patience she owned, Elizabeth smacked his ministering hand away and fixed him in place with an icy blue glare.

"The Lady Beaufort simply wishes for you to have the very best medical care, your grace," he said as though he was confused, but Elizabeth was sure that she saw a hint of amusement in his gentle, brown eyes.

She frowned. Directness was her preferred game, but Margaret had been working behind the scenes for years. "How does Henry fit into this?" Elizabeth blurted, seeing that her one link to the outside world was preparing to leave without imparting any greater knowledge.

Caerleon's face when he turned it to her expressed that he was impressed that she had worked out that much. Many people did not think of Henry Tudor, so long off in Brittany with no one besides his dedicated Uncle Jasper. The physician seemed pleased to see that Elizabeth knew what Margaret's motivation would be.

"I ask you again, your grace," he said softly. "What are your goals?"

Before she could answer him, Caerleon was gone again, and Elizabeth had to exert all her remaining willpower to keep from screaming at the empty room.

All Elizabeth could do was wait while anger and frustration bubbled within her. It was not enough to hope that the doctor would return with some concrete offer from Margaret Beaufort. She had a feeling that the delay was all part of the haughty countess' plan.

Elizabeth hated Margaret Beaufort and women like her. They looked down their noble noses at Elizabeth as if she had not been queen of England. She knew that they whispered that she was a commoner, as if her mother had not been married to the brother of King Henry V. But when Elizabeth had been married to Edward, it had not mattered. Nothing they could say had power over her then.

Unable to abide staying in bed any longer, Elizabeth moved to the window seat where she worked to untangle the hair that had once been her crowning glory. The silvery blonde color helped mask the grey that was sneaking into the strands, but she no longer cared. Her appearance could no longer get her what she wanted.

What did Margaret Beaufort want from her?

The question plagued her as she put on her melancholy act for her daughters in order to ensure that Caerleon would be called upon. Remaining melancholy was an easier task than staying abed. All Elizabeth had to do was remember the scheming Gloucester parading into London two months earlier, wearing the black of mourning for his brother while plotting his own rise behind that somber mask.

He now publicly wore purple. Fear wrapped its fingers around Elizabeth's heart when she thought of the small, dark man who was so unlike his older brother. Edward had always trusted and loved Richard, but Elizabeth knew that Richard's love for Edward had never extended to her.

A knock at the heavy oak door drew Elizabeth from her reverie. She realized that her hands were shaking, so she clutched them tightly together in her lap as she called for Bess to enter. A grin almost stole across her face when she saw that her daughter was not alone.

Instead, Elizabeth slouched and allowed weariness to encompass her features. One did not appear as loyal wife and queen to a philandering husband for as many years as Elizabeth had without gaining some dramatic skills. She could hear Bess making soft sounds of dismay but kept her eyes on the scene outside the window as if the doctor's presence interested her not one bit.

111

The eagerness inside her coalesced into nausea, and she prayed for Bess to leave the room. However, Bess seated herself on the edge of Elizabeth's bed and seemed intent to remain throughout the visit.

"No," Elizabeth said in dismay before realizing she had spoken aloud.

Bess appeared confused, while Caerleon gave no indication that he had heard. Elizabeth shook her head and bit her lip.

"Bess," she began again, attempting to sound sweet. "Please, leave me with the good doctor for a few moments that I may consult him privately."

Although her eyes widened slightly, Bess stood and walked slowly toward the door. Her searching look made clear that she worried only about what might be ailing her mother that could not be spoken in her presence, so Elizabeth put some poor effort into soothing her daughter's concerns with platitudes before the door shut behind her.

"You will not leave without telling me what I want to know this time," Elizabeth stated firmly, no longer caring that Bess could easily have still heard through the door.

"I had no intention of doing otherwise," the doctor stated calmly while he extracted tools from his bag.

"And you will do none of that," Elizabeth ordered as an afterthought. She was not truly melancholy and did not like how she felt after the bleeding was complete.

"Very well," he agreed though he continued to line up the items that should be used.

Summer sun spilled into the room, and Elizabeth felt a miniscule stirring of joy and anticipation before Caerleon spoke again.

"What made you decide to send Prince Richard to be with his brother?"

Elizabeth frowned and deep furrows appeared upon her brow. "What else could I do?" she snapped angrily. "The Duke of Gloucester has all the power and requested his presence. It would have only exacerbated the situation if I had attempted to deny him."

Nodding sadly, Caerleon lifted his gaze to look at Elizabeth directly for the first time. "I do not know if you will see your sons again."

Elizabeth's breath caught in her throat, and she wondered how a man who appeared so kindly could utter a damnable piece of information like that without so much as blinking. "What do you mean?" she whispered furiously.

He had moved close enough for her to smell the cloves on his breath, and his face held an intensity that it had not on previous visits. Elizabeth felt her stomach twist into knots before he even said the words.

"It is likely that the good duke intends to rid himself of the inconvenience of royal princes," Caerleon said, his eyes not moving from hers as if to be certain that she fully appreciated the truth of his statement.

Elizabeth leaned away to distance herself from the idea and swallowed the bile that threatened to rise in her throat. She did not immediately speak, but considered the possibility that he was right.

Richard had never demonstrated a trace of disloyalty with Edward, but would that devotion be transferred to his sons? Her sons? Suddenly, she hated herself for every dismissive or cutting comment she had made when she was so certain that her position was too high above the king's brother for him to ever retaliate.

"He would do no such thing," she stated more certainly than she felt.

Doctor Caerleon shrugged, his face losing the passion that had formerly inflamed it. He began meticulously returning tools to his bag.

"Wait!" Elizabeth cried. "I am ready to listen. Please!" She grabbed his arm frantically and wondered that she was begging this common man – a traitor to the crown no doubt – for mercy.

He looked down at her fingers, gripping tightly as they would a lover, and then returned his gaze to her anxious face. "There is much occurring that you are left unaware of," he said quietly. When she did not object or argue, he smiled faintly. Elizabeth felt as though she had been tamed but would not dare speak again until he had shared all he planned to impart.

"Richard plans to take the throne for himself," Caerleon began. "That is the reason for your children's bastardization, but he will depend upon an act of Parliament to secure his crown. Richard will see the need soon, if he does not already, to remove any other potential claimants, anyone rebellion could become centered upon."

Elizabeth was frozen in fear for her sons. She could not argue with Caerleon's logic. It is exactly what she would do. It was indeed what she had counselled Edward to do once he had Henry VI in his power and Prince Edouard was dead. Would God punish her children for the sins of their parents?

She went cold with dread, but would not give up. "What can I do?" she asked, her voice firm and giving life to none of the doubt growing within her.

"You can do nothing," he admitted. "But take heart that a rescue attempt will be made on your behalf."

He was already moving toward the door, and Elizabeth fought to sort through the questions racing through her mind. What if they did not succeed? Who could be trusted with such a mission? Where would her sons be taken?

"Why?" was all she managed. "Why is Margaret Beaufort helping me?"

For a moment, Elizabeth was sure that he was not going to answer, that he was going to leave her waiting again, but he paused with his hand on the latch of the door.

"Because Margaret Beaufort is also a mother who loves her son," he said, and was gone before Elizabeth could reply.

July 1483

From their safe but cramped quarters, Elizabeth heard the sounds of celebration. A heavy, sickening feeling started in her chest and spread until she feared it would overpower her. Those subjects who had seemed so faithful to Edward now ushered his brother into power, seemingly unconcerned that the former king's wife wasted away in sanctuary only a few steps away.

She yanked at her hair, which hung loose for she had little reason to have it tended. How could they, she wondered as she examined the handful of strands that had surrendered to her anger. Was there no one left in London concerned for her or her children?

Doctor Caerleon's words still sent a chill down her arms when she remembered them, but she could not bring herself to believe that her sons were lost to her. Elizabeth would never defend the actions of the Duke of Gloucester, now King of England, but even she could not believe him to be a child murderer.

With another merciless pull at her own hair, Elizabeth strode to the window, as if she might catch a glimpse of her brother-in-law and see the answers to her fears in his countenance or mannerisms. No longer a part of such festivities, Elizabeth could only imagine the coronation taking place within the abbey.

Richard and Anne were being crowned together, and the thought of the slim, frail woman taking her place as queen made Elizabeth tug again at her greying locks. Margaret Beaufort would be there, carrying Anne's train, an experience that was meant to be an honor but Elizabeth was certain had to be humiliating for her. A cruel snort of laughter escaped, and Elizabeth moved away from the window to sit heavily upon the edge of the bed.

Would Margaret help her sons escape from the Tower? She stilled her hands to keep them from thinning her hair even further as she questioned everything she knew. Could she really trust Margaret Beaufort?

Edward had left Henry Tudor, Margaret's only son, in exile throughout his reign. Elizabeth had supported this strategy, knowing Margaret's pride in her royal blood and limitless ambition. It seemed best to leave the Lancastrian pup across the water in Brittany. Would Margaret have greater compassion for Elizabeth's sons than Elizabeth had offered Henry?

A knock made Elizabeth gasp as she jumped from the bed. Shaking her head clear, she opened the door to her eldest daughter, Bess, who carried a wriggling Bridget in her arms.

"Mama, would you come out and read with us?" Bess requested as Bridget stretched her arms out pleadingly to their mother.

Elizabeth ignored the whimpering child but glanced into the next room where her daughters were employed by studies and embroidery. Each one's studiousness evinced that they had been schooled to not mention the coronation of their uncle. A whisper of a smile crossed Elizabeth's features. These children might be the only people left in the world who cared for her.

"Of course, I will," she sighed, finally taking Bridget from Bess' weary arms. "It will do me good to spend time with my girls and away from my dreary thoughts."

The bright cheer on Bess' face was Elizabeth's reward for resigning herself to the domestic scene. Bridget clung so tightly that Elizabeth had to shift her weight to loosen the girl's grip upon her neck. Cecily stood eagerly when she saw that their mother had been beckoned from her private quarters.

"Can I get anything for you, mama?" Cecily said, bouncing in anticipation in a way that only a fourteen-year-old girl can. "Would you like to read from your book of hours?" she asked without giving Elizabeth time to respond before moving toward the trunk of books.

"Not right now," Elizabeth quickly halted her. She was in no mood for prayer. Looking at Bridget to avoid Cecily's disappointed face, she continued, "I think I will simply enjoy some time with my lovely daughters."

Cecily looked somewhat mollified as she took up her embroidery from where she had carelessly discarded it. "Alright, mama," she said with reduced enthusiasm. "I do enjoy listening to you read the prayers to us though."

"Later," Elizabeth dismissed her, turning her attention to Bess. "You seem to have something to say," she observed, making her daughter blush prettily.

Bess smoothed her skirts and took her seat before responding. When she did again raise her eyes to her mother's, there was pleading in them.

"Could we leave sanctuary now that our Uncle Richard is king?" she asked in a voice as soft as a sea breeze.

Elizabeth could tell that the girl wished to look away, so she pinned her more firmly with her gaze. "You think now would be a good time to leave?" she said, allowing doubtfulness to drip from her words. "Now that Richard has stolen your brothers' inheritance....now it must be safe to put ourselves at his mercy?"

Bess did not answer immediately, and Elizabeth realized that her grip upon Bridget was becoming dangerously firm while waiting. She released the child and stared at Bess, who calmly took Bridget onto her own lap before replying.

"We cannot reverse an act of Parliament," Bess said reasonably as she wiped tears from Bridget's face that Elizabeth had not noticed were there. "Richard is king. Shall we remain in sanctuary throughout his reign? Perhaps if we were to demonstrate our trust in him, he would reciprocate by reuniting us with my brothers."

Narrowing her eyes, Elizabeth considered this course. Could Bess be right? Even if she was, what future could her daughters have as bastard princesses under the power of their usurping uncle? How she wished she had a way of discovering just what Margaret Beaufort was planning! Trusting in the countess' vague promises seemed like her best strategy for now.

"I will consider it," Elizabeth said to buy herself time with her daughters. They were itching to leave the abbot's rooms just as much as she was, but it was her duty to consider what would come next. Simply trusting in Richard was not a viable option.

Later that month, she had reason to, once again, doubt herself. An amateurish attempt to free the princes from the Tower made Elizabeth wonder if she could have made a difference had she not been trapped in her voluntary prison.

Her anger boiled at Margaret Beaufort. A failed rescue attempt did nothing but ensure that the boys would be completely inaccessible from then on. Richard might not even leave them in London. All this flashed through Elizabeth's mind in the time it took Caerleon to needlessly assemble his tools on the table near Elizabeth's chair.

"I apologize that the news is not more favorable," he said, taking a small knife in his hand only to be used if Bess entered the room.

Staring at the collection of tools, Elizabeth wondered if he was truly sorry or if she and her sons were just pieces in the game of chess that Margaret was playing. Terror gripped her heart at the thought of her boys at the mercy of so many who might wish them harm. She did not enjoy the luxuries of complete information or time to decide what was prudent. Pushing her fear away, Elizabeth fixed Caerleon with a bold stare.

"What can I do?"

For the first time since he had begun his visits to the dowager queen in sanctuary, Caerleon looked at her with trust in his eyes. Elizabeth felt a tingle of anticipation. He would not leave her with partial answers and hints of plans this time. She grasped his hand and was surprised at its smoothness.

"I am ready to consider Margaret my full partner," Elizabeth vowed, unaware of her fingers unconsciously stroking his soft palm until Caerleon's eyes fell to their linked hands.

Pulling away, Elizabeth felt a flush rise to her cheeks, and she wondered how long it had been since a man had made her blush. Her eyes searched Caerleon more carefully. There was more to the unprepossessing physician than appeared at first glance. Elizabeth realized how lonely and desperate she was as she gazed into his warm brown eyes.

"She will be happy to hear that," he said in a firm voice, breaking the spell that Elizabeth had an awkward feeling only affected her. "Are you ready to demonstrate your devotion?" he asked.

Elizabeth nodded wordlessly, wondering how he had suddenly acquired the power to leave her speechless. Surely, it was her fears for her sons that left her choked up, not the way Caerleon's dark hair curled at his temples begging to be tamed.

He leaned in closer. Was he unaware of the effect he was having on her, or was he well aware and using it to his advantage? Elizabeth did not mind. She would have employed the same tactic.

"Henry Tudor is ready to return to his homeland," he whispered.

Furrowing her brow, Elizabeth did not deign to speak. This was nothing new. Margaret had been lobbying for Henry's pardon for over a decade.

"He will need a proper bride," Caerleon added, seeing Elizabeth's confusion.

The moment her brow cleared as realization struck, he leaned back with a satisfied smile stretched across his face. Elizabeth felt her jaw drop and forced her mouth closed. Her eyes automatically went to the door, as if the thought of her would bring Bess into the room. One side of her mouth curled up in ironic respect. Margaret did aim high.

"What does Bess get out of this?" she demanded, straightening her spine and freezing her features as if in ice. Now was not a time to be softened by a man's deceitful charm.

Caerleon's smile did not fade. "She will be queen," he said casually, as if the outcome should have been obvious.

Elizabeth struggled to keep any emotion from her countenance. How had Margaret hatched such an audacious idea? With her mind racing to calculate how it could possibly work, Elizabeth kept her eyes locked on Caerleon's. He gave no sign of distress, and it was Elizabeth who finally bit her lip in frustration.

"How?" she gave in and asked.

She had not realized it was possible for his smile to broaden. The lines from his eyes met that tempting curl at his temple, and he leaned forward in eagerness again.

"The people love Princess Elizabeth," he informed her unnecessarily. She was more than aware of how much more beloved her daughter was than herself. "The joint claim of her royal blood and Henry's will end the dispute between Lancaster and York and topple the shaky throne of Richard of Gloucester."

"She has been bastardized," Elizabeth pointed out just as unnecessarily, but Caerleon waved the objection away.

"An act of Parliament to be reversed upon their accession."

He made it sound easy, but Elizabeth knew that it would not be. "Richard is a stalwart warrior. Henry is not. How does he plan to defeat him?" she asked, keeping her guard up.

Caerleon shook his head ruefully and moved to stand. "You are still underestimating Margaret Beaufort."

"Wait!" Elizabeth cried. She grasped his arms in her hands and forced him to remain seated across from her. "You cannot leave me in uncertainty again."

She hated the pleading sound of her voice as much as the smugly satisfied look on his face, but she could not bear for them to part ways with things so unsettled between them.

"There is no uncertainty," he countered. "Just your decision. Will you make Bess a queen?"

Elizabeth cringed at his familiar reference to her daughter but had more serious concerns. Could she plot to crown her daughter in place of the son who had been raised to be king?

"You need time to consider your options, such as they are," Caerleon observed, standing despite her efforts to keep him in place. He expertly evaded her grasping hands to stand just outside her reach. "Do not worry," he added, seeing the distress in her eyes. "I will return, and the offer will stand. I cannot expect you to make a decision like this without proper prayer and contemplation."

Elizabeth breathed in deeply as she stood to face him. "Thank you," she said softly. "You have been a friend to me when all others have fled."

He took up her hand and kissed it softly, his warmth lingering after he released it. Elizabeth gently touched the spot after the door had latched behind him. Realizing what she was doing, she flung her hands apart and paced the room in frustration, her movements stirring up dust and the scent of rushes beyond their prime.

"Prayer!" she muttered to herself. That may be Margaret's strategy, but practical logic was hers. Was the best option available to her and her children that Bess be consort to a Tudor king? Surely not, but what else could she do?

August 1483

Elizabeth agonized over whether to betroth Bess to Henry Tudor, a man she would have never considered for any of her daughters a few months ago. She had to keep reminding herself that Edward was not going to suddenly arrive to save the day. Caerleon had been gone an excruciatingly long time, but Elizabeth was thankful, for his return meant that she would have to commit to her next step, as uncertain as she was of what it should be.

The sounds of horses and men outside made her blood run cold. This was it. In a moment, Caerleon would walk in and demand her answer. Her eyes frantically searched the room for the answer that continued to elude her. Lift up her daughter or hold out hope for her son? What mother could choose?

She had begun to pull at her hair, dry strands breaking off in her fingers, when a voice from outside captivated her attention. Her visitor was not Caerleon after all, and Elizabeth's fear was swept away by curiosity just as the door opened to reveal, not the mild mannered physician, but the jocular Duke of Buckingham.

Elizabeth stood and blurted, "Harry, what are you doing here?"

He was a mountain of a man, easily recognizable as Edward's cousin, with russet curls and ruddy cheeks. He stomped his feet as he came in as if he was so used to winter snow and spring mud that the habit stayed with him throughout the year. Before responding to her, Harry flashed Elizabeth a disarming grin that made her miss Edward more than ever. However, her trust for the ambitious duke did not match that she had held for her husband. Without returning his smile, she repeated her inquiry.

"What are you doing here?" she demanded, letting her frozen features convey her resolution to not be taken in by his charm.

With a final smoothing of his tunic and hand run carelessly

through his already tousled hair, he answered, "I am here to help, of course."

Elizabeth's raised eyebrow was her only response. She did not remember Harry Stafford ever helping anyone besides himself. Edward had not trusted him, and neither would she. Still, as he elegantly bowed before her and kissed her hand, she did wish that she had been more disciplined with her beauty routine since entering sanctuary.

"You will be currently trying to decide if your future hope lies with your son or your daughter," he said casually as he drew himself to his full height.

At this Elizabeth could no longer control her countenance. Her eyes widened, and she wondered if she had underestimated the duke.

Without waiting for her to respond, Harry filled a goblet from a nearby sideboard and took up the room's most comfortable chair. Settled, he looked to her in eagerness.

Elizabeth found herself stammering and despised her own weakness. "I am sure that I do not know what you mean." She forced confidence into her voice and held her head high. "My son will be king like his father before him."

Now the emotion that Elizabeth trusted even less than charm took over Buckingham's face. Pity.

"Surely, you do not still hold out hope in that regard?"

Angrily pulling at her hair as she took a seat across from him, she argued, "I have little choice remaining to me."

"Ah, but there is where you are wrong," he insisted, leaning toward her. "Quite wrong."

Elizabeth refused to meet his gaze. What did he know and how did he know it?

He leaned back, took a sip from his cup, and offered her another lopsided grin. "I know exactly what you are thinking. Do you know that? You think that you are the untouchable Elizabeth Woodville, outsmarting everyone and always getting your way." His smile disappeared and features hardened. "But you are wrong this time, your grace." The snide tone he used for her royal title told her just what he thought of her status. "You will be ruling nothing from this moment forward. If you have not already learned that, accept it now."

To her great horror, she felt the sharp heat of tears threatening to spill from her eyes. His words hurt all the more because she knew them to be true. She no longer had her youthful beauty that had enabled her to manipulate a king, and she had made too many enemies believing that Edward would always protect her from any enemy.

"You said you were here to help," Elizabeth snapped, still hiding her face behind the fall of her uncombed hair.

"And that I am," Harry agreed, his voice again kind. "The decision you are attempting to make is easier than you believe."

"There is nothing that could make this situation easier," she scoffed.

He leaned toward her again and lowered his voice. "I said the decision was simplified, not the situation." Seeing confusion in her face when she finally looked at him, he continued, "Your only hope in this world is your daughter. Do not hold out hope for your sons."

Elizabeth felt her heart grow cold and heavy, and the sensation spread throughout her body as her mind took in his meaning.

"What has happened to Edward and Richard?" she demanded through clenched teeth.

Buckingham examined her features as if deciding how to choose his next words. In the end, he seemed to decide to be as harsh as he believed Elizabeth would have been if their positions were reversed.

"They are dead."

The sentence seemed to echo through the eerie silence that followed it. Elizabeth's fidgeting fingers fell from her hair and clutched together in her lap. She bit her lip and blinked rapidly. Yet, at the same time, she discovered that she was not completely shocked. The realization struck her painfully that Buckingham had simply confirmed a truth that she had long suspected but prayed would be proven false.

"Leave."

Elizabeth stood and swept from the room without another word. She would not give him the satisfaction of observing her raw grief. Therefore, she did not realize that he remained in the room long after she had slammed the door to her sleeping quarters, long enough to hear her shriek and scream as she pulled out her hair and melted to the floor in her sorrow.

October 1483

If it were possible, time slowed down for Elizabeth after Harry Stafford's revelation. Though he said her strategy should now be obvious, she was still uncertain about what to do. Word had been sent through Caerleon that Elizabeth was prepared to support Margaret Beaufort and betroth their children.

Meanwhile, her daughters continued to press her for her permission to leave sanctuary. They naively trusted their Uncle Richard and were weary of staying hidden away. Nothing could be done about events of the past. They were young women and wished to make lives for themselves beyond this cloistered existence.

Even when Elizabeth broke down and told Bess that the boys were dead – Richard had killed them – the girl had refused to listen. Elizabeth shook her head at the memory. Bess would never believe her, yet what could she do but place her family at Richard's mercy?

No. Not yet. First, she would have her assurance from Margaret that Henry Tudor would fulfill his side of their bargain. A crown for Bess. She would accept nothing less.

A visit from her brother-in-law, now King Richard, took her by surprise, as did his disheveled appearance. He wasted no time on pleasantries.

"It is time for you to drop this charade and leave sanctuary," he said, twisting the rings shimmering with jewels on his fingers.

Elizabeth examined the man her husband had trusted without hesitation. His brother, Richard, was average sized with dark hair where Edward had been tall with light auburn locks. Richard was devout and intellectual, characteristics no one would have accused Edward of displaying. What they had in common was ambition and skill on the field of battle. What Richard lacked in physique, he made up for in clever strategy.

Was killing her sons just another brilliant move to secure his own success? She found herself cringing from his closeness.

"I know you have been scheming with the Duke of Buckingham," Richard announced when she failed to speak.

Smoothly controlling her reaction, Elizabeth countered lightly, "I know little of the duke's actions or plans. What on earth could I have to discuss with him?"

Richard locked his gaze on her as he seemed to consider and reject several replies. "He finds himself accused of conspiring against the crown," he finally said.

It was difficult to keep from gulping down the lump that grew in her throat, but Elizabeth maintained eye contact for long enough to profess her innocence before shrugging.

"Edward never trusted him. I suppose you should not have either."

She felt his eyes follow her as she strolled to the window as if she could not care less what happened to the Duke of Buckingham.

"Maybe you are right," he conceded, and Elizabeth heard him collapse into the nearest chair.

Her forehead furrowed. What game was he playing? She turned, but Richard was no longer looking at her. His head was in his hands, and he looked defeated.

"I believe I did trust Buckingham too much. Far too much," he said, rubbing his face wearily. When his eyes found her again, he seemed surprised that she was still there. "That being in the past," he continued, "I would like to do what I can to secure your daughters' futures."

She almost laughed, but controlled the reaction into a sarcastic sneer. Like he had secured her sons' futures? "As their mother, I believe that responsibility falls to me," she replied.

"And is that what you are doing by keeping them here?" he asked with a sweeping gesture that encompassed the dark room with furnishings that were practical but not luxurious. Her daughters did not complain, but the abbey was far from equal to the life they were accustomed to.

"They must be lonely," Richard added, as if reading her mind. "They are young and wish to be with other young people."

"And we are an embarrassment to you," Elizabeth could not resist adding.

Richard sighed and massaged the nape of his neck. "There is no use denying it," he admitted. "The fact that you remain here does complicate things."

"As did the existence of my sons!"

Elizabeth's hand flew to her mouth. The words had escaped before she could stop them, but she was shocked to see that Richard appeared more confused than convicted.

"Their illegitimacy was through no fault of mine," he insisted, standing as he spoke. "You need more time. I shall grant it, but do try to see that I want what is best for your family and the kingdom."

His quick stride carried him from the room before Elizabeth could decide what his unexpected reaction had implied.

Her sons were dead. Were they not?

Elizabeth moved through the borrowed rooms in a daze. Each time she felt certain of what she must do, some new fog draped over the future to make her doubt herself. Were it only her own fate in question, she could confidently plunge on, but hesitation grasped at her heart where her children were concerned.

So caught up in weighing Buckingham's versus Richard's words was she that she failed to notice Cecily's approach until they nearly collided.

"Mother," Cecily said in a conspiratorial whisper. "Did Richard tell you about Buckingham?"

The girl had gripped her mother's arm and pulled her into a small alcove though there was no one nearby to observe them.

Confusion marred Elizabeth's features as she tried to determine how Cecily read her thoughts.

"Tell me what?" she asked in frustration. Elizabeth could not get used to this feeling of being an outsider in the kingdom that had so recently been hers.

Cecily's fingers dug into her mother's arm in what could have been fear or excitement as she cried, "He has been arrested!"

Elizabeth felt her blood turn to ice. Had Richard been toying with her, pretending innocence to encourage traitorous words from her?

"Where did you hear this?" she demanded of her daughter.

"The same way we hear anything," Cecily said, instinctively pulling away from her mother's intensity, "the servants."

"What has he been charged with?" As she asked, Elizabeth wondered how many people knew that Harry had visited her. Would his guilt incriminate her or her children? Before she could consider the consequences, Cecily answered.

"Treason."

Elizabeth fell against the wall, her muscles weakened in dread and her bones feeling as though they had turned to dust. What hope was there now, she wondered, just as Cecily provided it.

"It is said that he rebelled to make a way for Tudor. Some believe that he has already landed in Wales."

And at that moment Elizabeth knew. Margaret Beaufort and her son, Henry Tudor, were her path forward. Buckingham could be sacrificed. Margaret's network had deep enough roots to be rid of the boisterous and incautious duke. Elizabeth looked at her daughter's face and saw concern plainly written there.

"My dear," she said laying a hand on Cecily's soft cheek, "could you see that the doctor is summoned. Suddenly, I am not feeling well."

December 1483

Once she had determined her course, Elizabeth would not stray from it. Doctor Caerleon assured her that everything was in place, and Elizabeth had sent her son, Thomas, to officially support Henry Tudor as he prepared to steal Richard's crown. All that remained was to inform Bess of her role.

Elizabeth felt more like her old self as she waited for Bess to join her in her room. The past months had been a greater tribulation that she had ever expected to face at this point in her life, but she had survived. They would do better than survive. Her daughter would reclaim what was rightly hers.

When Bess entered, beautiful but demure, Elizabeth had just an inkling of doubt. She prayed that Bess had the stamina to do what needed to be done.

"I have wonderful news for you!" Elizabeth gushed, ignoring the look of concern and doubt that lined Bess' features.

"What is it?" Bess asked, and Elizabeth took her hands in the hope that her own enthusiam might be contagious.

"A betrothal for you, my darling," Elizabeth cried happily. Any remaining questions she had about Tudor must be deeply buried. She had to confidently present this to Bess as the best choice. Their only choice.

To her great disappointment, Bess pulled away. She seemed to be put off by her mother's excitement rather than catching it.

"How could you have negotiated a marriage while we remain self-enforced prisoners?" Bess demanded angrily as she spun to face her mother. "And to who?"

Elizabeth took a calming breath and kept her face arranged in matronly happiness. Moving to place her hands on Bess' shoulders, she prayed for Bess to accept the plan she had already set in motion. The distrust in her eldest daughter's eyes almost broke her resolve. Almost.

"With Henry Tudor, my daughter. He is Lancaster's final red rose, and the two of you will unite the warring factions."

Yes, she thought to herself. Emphasize the bringing of peace. Elizabeth knew that Bess had come of age surrounded by war and would do anything to stop it, including marrying Henry Tudor.

Bess reached clumsily for the closest bench and fell onto it, shaking her head in exasperation. Elizabeth was trying to form her next words, those that would help Bess accept her fate when the girl unexpectedly lashed out.

"How could you? What do you mean warring factions? Father crushed the Lancastrians and Henry Tudor is in exile!"

Bess looked like she was going to be sick, and Elizabeth had never heard her so angry. In all her calculations, she had never considered that Bess would be a stumbling block. The girl was normally so submissive and pliable. Much as it made her heart ache, Elizabeth knew that it was time to remind her daughter who was in charge.

"Your father is no longer here to keep him in exile though, is he?" Elizabeth controlled her face to appear as though she had scored a point. She could not allow her daughter to see that her heart, too, was still broken by Edward's absence. She would never have had to stoop to marrying her daughter to Tudor if Edward were yet alive.

Bess looked disgusted by her mother's words. "You plan to rebel against your husband's brother, the man he named Protector of the Realm?"

She asked it in such innocence, and Elizabeth wondered how this could be a daughter of hers. Or of Edward's for that matter. They had both understood that some distasteful actions must be undertaken to reach a higher goal.

"It is the only way," she insisted in a quiet but firm voice.

Bess looked around the room as though searching for

answers. "But Edward is the one who should be king, if not Richard. Do you think Henry is going to invade and then hand the crown over to my brother?"

So naïve, Elizabeth thought. She thought of Buckingham, his head struck from his body the month before and knew in that moment that Richard had not spared her sons. Accepting this truth was the only way she could do what she must.

"Edward is dead," she said with such certainty that she hoped Bess would accept it, for speaking on it further would break her heart. But Bess was not calmly trusting her word.

"How can you say that? Surely my uncle has simply had Edward and Richard moved to some more appropriate residence," Bess insisted with all the passion of a young woman who wants nothing more than to believe what she has said.

Elizabeth wished with all her heart that she could believe it too....but she did not. She felt anger rise in her that Bess could believe her guilty of choosing this plan of action if she believed either of her sons were alive. Her next words were fueled by that fury and all the pain of the preceding months.

"Do you hear yourself? You naïve girl!"

Elizabeth paced the room, horrified by her inability to control her emotions. The dust stirred from the rushes caught in her nostrils and made her eyes water. The tears came easily as she thought of her sons and what their last moments might have been like. Had they felt abandoned by their mother? She was so lost in her own nightmarish thoughts, that she almost missed Bess' quiet, deadly barb.

"Do you hear yourself?"

In order to hear the whispered words, Elizabeth had to still her frantic movements and hope the girl did not notice her tears.

"You calmly state that your sons are dead at the hand of our uncle, the king. Yet you do not mourn them, but look for a way for me to supplant them with this creature Tudor."

Did not mourn them? Is that what the selfish girl thought? Elizabeth felt her face grow hot with all the grief and anger that she was forced to endure behind a queenly mask. She did not realize that she was raising her hand to her daughter until it had almost struck her pale cheek. Elizabeth looked at her hand, hating herself as she dropped it to her side.

She could not meet her daughter's eye but heard her parting words with painful clarity.

"Once again, I know the truth from what you do not say rather than what you do. You did not deny father's precontract, and now you do not deny that you scheme against your own sons to replace them with their sister, only because you hope for more power for yourself that way."

The daggers struck home, and Elizabeth found she could not speak as the sound of her daughter's footsteps retreated behind the slammed door.

She had been queen of England. She had secured everything she had ever wanted for herself and her family. Now it was all crumbling apart, and even her own daughter did not believe in her. All of Elizabeth's pride and confidence evaporated in that moment as hot tears raced down her face. Maybe, if Bess had not rushed away quite so quickly, she would have been touched by the sound of her mother's sobbing.

March 1484

Word reached them that Henry Tudor had stood in Rennes Cathedral on Christmas Day and announced his betrothal to Elizabeth of York. Bess was horrified and pleaded with her mother to leave sanctuary that they might more effectively seek the truth. While Elizabeth was certain that she had already discerned the truth for herself, she also had decided that it was time to rejoin the outside world.

The only revenge she could have on her brother-in-law for the time being was to force him to make an embarrassing public promise to protect and care for her daughters. It brought Elizabeth some small measure of pleasure, until she pictured the faces of her dear sons now lost to her. No public humiliation could make up for their deaths.

Preparing to leave the familiar abbot's rooms made Elizabeth think about her sons and how their presence would be missing from her life. While in sanctuary it was easy to fool herself into thinking they were simply somewhere else, the way Bess did. However, once they attempted to begin what would now pass for a normal life, their places would be agonizingly vacant.

She could not understand why, as grief gripped her heart anew at the thought of going on with life without her husband and sons, her daughters were jovial. Bess and Cecily whispered about potential dance partners and modern fashions. The younger girls daydreamed about sweetmeats and roasts they would taste at court. The thought of feasting at King Richard's side made Elizabeth's insides churn and bubble.

A shiver of terror ran though Elizabeth's body as they stepped out of the abbey. The sunlight was stunning, though it did not provide sufficient warmth, but the world held dangers and fears for her that she had never formerly concerned herself with. She felt like a mother fox taking her babies onto a grassy field surrounded by hounds.

Richard had come to greet them, and the sight of him revolted her. How could he face her so blithely with the knowledge of what he had done? She wondered if he had always served Edward as loyally as her husband had believed. Seeing the way Richard could so convincingly charm her daughters, she wondered if Edward had not also been caught in his trap.

Scents of spring filled the air, and Elizabeth had missed the fragrance of fresh greenery and new life. However, all she could think of as she watched Bess take Richard's arm was that Henry Tudor had better come. And soon.

September 1484

Six months had passed since Elizabeth had allowed herself to be convinced to put her daughters in Richard's care. She was frustrated and felt foolish. On one hand, the fact that her daughters were content and seemed to be safe reassured her. On the other, it made herself doubt, once again, what Buckingham had told her about her sons.

Communication with Margaret Beaufort had to be cautiously carried out. Buckingham's rebellion had incriminated her as well, since it was well known that Henry Tudor had also been preparing to attack at that time. When Richard's only son had died in April, Elizabeth had been surprised that Tudor failed to press his advantage.

Richard was a grief-stricken king without heir. How could Tudor have let the summer campaigning season pass without exposing the king's vulnerabilities?

Elizabeth decided it was time to speak with Margaret herself. Having no official title or duties, Elizabeth lived on the edges of court where nobody paid her any mind. It was therefore a simple task to arrange a trip to visit Margaret at Lathom.

The castle was more of a fortress than Margaret's preferred estate at Woking, but technically the countess remained under house arrest. That her husband was her gaolor indicated the king's lack of concern for female conspirators. The thought was one of the few that made Elizabeth smile. Little did he know.

A surprising level of nervousness overcame Elizabeth as she approached the gilded prison. She had known Margaret only from the superior position as her queen and wondered how she would maintain her authority with the imperious woman now that many referred to Elizabeth simply as Lady Grey.

Pulling back her shoulders, Elizabeth reminded herself that Margaret still needed her daughter. Her enemies might claim that she was no wife of King Edward, but they still loved Princess Bess. She would not let Margaret intimidate her.

Such was easier said than done when the woman was before her. Margaret Beaufort, now Margaret Stanley, was a diminutive woman who managed to seem a much larger presence than she truly was. Her arrow-thin form spoke of a different form of strength than that the men brought to the field of battle. Elizabeth studied her former lady-in-waiting, and Margaret did not cower or blush under examination.

Margaret's severe style of dress made her appear years older than her true age, and Elizabeth wondered, as only a woman who had been married to a man years younger than herself can, why on earth anyone would choose to do so. The deep emerald of her gown was almost black, and her hair was pulled back so tightly Elizabeth felt certain that it must make her head ache. The rings on her tiny fingers were her only ornamentation.

Elizabeth felt somewhat gaudy in comparison. Anxious to maintain the upper hand and retain what she could of her former royal status, she had dressed elaborately in bright fabrics and sparkling jewels. Margaret's eyes seemed to take this all in and dismiss it as unimportant in an instant.

Settling into seats that had been prepared for them in a private room, Margaret did not waste time on trivial matters. She handed Elizabeth a goblet holding a small measure of wine as she asked in a clipped voice, "You intend to honor our agreement?"

Elizabeth had raised the cup to her mouth before lowering it in surprise.

"Of course. Why would I not?"

Margaret narrowed her eyes at Elizabeth as if determining how much to say or wondering how much Elizabeth already knew. It made Elizabeth nervous, for suddenly she realized that almost everything she thought she knew had come from this woman whose priorities were not her own.

Margaret nodded to herself, seeming to have decided something and answered, "Your girls spend their days at the court of their uncle."

Rather than justify her decision, Elizabeth countered with her own question. "Where would they be better placed at this time?"

Raising her eyebrows slightly, Margaret accepted this answer and took a sip of her wine before continuing.

"Bess is prepared to serve Henry?" she asked.

Elizabeth balked at the idea of her eldest daughter submitting to the exiled boy, but she kept her smile firmly in place.

"When they are married, they will rule well and bring lasting peace."

Was that a slight upturn to Margaret's lips? They seemed to enjoy avoiding each other's questions.

"She accepts the betrothal then?" Margaret prodded. She would not risk her son on an uncommitted ally.

"Bess does as she is commanded," Elizabeth snapped before realizing that she was indeed painting her daughter as a submissive consort rather than ruling queen. Her lips pressed together into a thin line. "When will Henry be coming to claim his bride?" she asked in order to shift the conversation to the deficiencies of Margaret's child rather than those of her own.

"Buckingham moved too quickly. Everything had been put in place, but Buckingham was too eager to appear the hero. Instead, he died a traitor, and Richard still does not even know the half of it." Margaret stopped abruptly, as if she realized that she was saying too much, then continued more calmly, "Henry will come."

Sipping her wine to buy time, Elizabeth considered. What did Richard not know? What did she not know? Why would Harry have sacrificed himself for Henry Tudor? She could ask none of these questions.

She settled for asking, "When?"

Most people would shift uneasily when asked such a pointed, difficult question. Margaret Beaufort did not lower her eyes or move a muscle.

"When his success is certain, of course."

"Are my sons dead?" Elizabeth had asked it without thinking. It was as if the spirit of one of her daughters had compelled her with their own uncertainty.

"Why would you question it?" Margaret asked with an odd bemused look, almost a smile, on her face.

"Buckingham said so, but Richard has given me doubt," she admitted, unsure of whether she was exposing too much of her own weakness to this cold, controlled woman.

"No one was better acquainted with the fate of your sons than Harry Stafford," Margaret said, and now Elizabeth was certain that it was a peculiar smile being repressed.

Elizabeth's brow furrowed at the enigmatic words and the expression that nudged her to come to the right conclusion. Horror came over her as she realized what Margaret was saying.

"Did Harry murder my boys?" Elizabeth whispered.

At the raw emotion in Elizabeth's voice and countenance, Margaret seemed to regain control of herself. The eerie grin was replaced by a frozen lack of emotion.

"I have reason to believe that he did," Margaret confessed before adding as an afterthought, "I am sorry for your great loss. God grant you comfort."

This was not making sense. Elizabeth fought the urge to stand and pace or to run outside and be alone with her thoughts. She could not process this information under Margaret's studious gaze.

"But Buckingham served Richard. Did he hope to gain the

throne for himself?" She looked at the younger woman and saw the emotion that she despised most. She would have none of Margaret Beaufort's pity. "Did he do it for Henry?"

The shock that had crossed Margaret's face was quickly composed, but Elizabeth had witnessed it long enough to have the pieces fall into place in her mind.

Buckingham knew her sons were dead because he had killed them. He had killed them to clear the way for Henry Tudor. He had done it at Margaret's command. In the meantime, Margaret had convinced Elizabeth to betroth her daughter, now heir to the kingdom, to this last Lancastrian upstart.

How could she have been so stupid?

Margaret had composed herself and was attempting to keep Elizabeth from reaching this conclusion.

"Buckingham must have done it on King Richard's orders," she insisted almost frantically. "Or if not on his orders, so to ease his burden. This has nothing to do with Henry."

But Elizabeth knew better. For Margaret, everything had to do with Henry. She could see the plan forming together in her mind. How she wished she had seen it sooner! Together, Margaret and Harry had plotted and killed her sons.

When she remembered the confusion on Richard's face, she realized how incapable he would have been of duplicity. However, Elizabeth knew of someone else who was more than capable of that sort of betrayal....and she had betrothed her daughter to that woman's son.

March 1485

The note to Thomas was tightly clutched in Elizabeth's hand. She had underestimated the difficulty in getting word to him at Tudor's court of exiles without using Margaret's couriers. Cursing herself once again for the trust she had placed in that ambitious woman, Elizabeth turned the note over along with a ridiculously heavy sack of coin that was the required payment for seeing it delivered.

She hoped that she was not too late.

How could she have been so foolish? She had been blinded by grief and anger. She had left herself trapped within the walls of sanctuary for too long, where only news that people want one to receive can reach. It had been Margaret, not Richard, all along. Now she was sure of it, and Elizabeth's only remaining son served hers.

Piety did not come naturally to Elizabeth as it did to Bess, but after she watched the messenger gallop away she prayed like she never had before in her life. Let the message find Thomas, and let him find a way to escape. She could not lose a fourth son to these battles for the crown.

If Thomas came home and Richard defeated Henry on the field, should the coward ever actually land on England's shores, Elizabeth could be content. She may not have always done the right thing, but she could manage to protect those she had left.

At least she could breathe easy where her daughters were concerned. Bess had been accepted into the household of Richard's queen. Anne Neville was a submissive creature who adored her husband. She may not be the type of woman Elizabeth much admired, but Bess would be content and well-protected at her side.

The two had even worn matching gowns for the Christmas festivities at court a few months earlier. Elizabeth was, of course, aware of the rumors that whispered Richard's hopes of marrying sweet, young Bess himself, but even Elizabeth found that preposterous. She had known Richard and Anne too long to believe either of them capable of disloyalty. However, she also recognized that Anne was seriously ill. If Anne were out of the picture, would Richard protect Bess from Henry by marrying her himself? Knowing her daughter as she did, Elizabeth was certain that Bess would be more open to that betrothal than the one currently arranged for her.

Life had not gained predictability as Elizabeth aged, and she smirked at the belief of her younger self that life would be easy once she was queen. Too many unanswered questioned plagued her now. Would Henry attack? Could he win?

Elizabeth Woodville clutched her rosary beads and prayed as she never had before.

August 1485

Elizabeth had watched Richard's troops as they marched out of the city weeks earlier in response to the news that Tudor planned an attack. When it would occur or where exactly they would attempt to land had been unknown at that time, so the king had stationed himself at a central location to wait.

She had sometimes envied the power that men could wield, but as Elizabeth envisioned the mental strain and physical exhaustion of an army camp waiting upon an enemy she had reason to be thankful that she had been born a woman.

Then the news had arrived.

It struck Elizabeth like a physical blow. Richard defeated. Henry king. The fact that she had played a part in this macabre production made bile rise in her throat.

What about Bess?

Elizabeth's thin hands shook and pulled at her silvery blonde hair as the realization slowly settled upon her like a blanket of snow falling on spring flowers that had bloomed too early. Bess would have to marry him, the son of the woman who had schemed to kill her brothers.

"There is no other way," Elizabeth announced to the empty room. She and her remaining children had no choice but to make themselves a vital part of the Tudor regime.

Pacing frantically, Elizabeth voiced her worst fears, "What if Bess discovers the truth?"

As the scent of lavender rose into the stuffy room, stirred from the rushes by Elizabeth's constant motion, she knew the answer. Bess could never know, and Elizabeth would have to pretend that she did not either.

The only possibility now was for Bess to make a successful marriage with Henry Tudor and never know that her brothers had been murdered to clear the way for him.

Elizabeth halted her agitated movements as a thought struck her, and she whispered, "Does Henry even know?"

September 1485

Elizabeth lightly touched her fingers to her smooth hair and fine gown. She had played many roles throughout her turbulent life, but none could compare to this.

It had become almost immediately clear to her that her daughters' futures required embracing Henry Tudor. He was the best hope for her family. She would keep Margaret's secret and pray that their children proved better for the kingdom than their mothers had been.

She stood in the hall of Coldharbour House, a fittingly named estate for the king's mother. Soon, Bess would arrive and Elizabeth would be required to act as though this was everything she had wanted, everything she had planned. Bess would never guess the truth.

Margaret approached with an unassuming man. By the adoring gaze that he received from the mistress of Coldharbour, Elizabeth knew that this must be her daughter's betrothed.

Henry did not hold himself proudly the way Edward had. No, Edward had been born to be king - tall, strong, and glorious. This man had a quiet confidence, but none of the bold arrogance her husband had embodied. With a tiny shake of her head, Elizabeth banished all thoughts of her dead husband from her mind. He could not help her now.

She curtseyed low before King Henry VII, who quickly raised her up as if embarrassed by the act of obeisance. His hands were rough and his face somewhat weathered. He had not been raised with the comforts of one intended to rule, but his eyes shone with an intelligence that Elizabeth guessed many people underestimated.

"Your grace," he was kind enough to address her as a queen rather than as the whore that Richard had branded her. Elizabeth felt her heart melt slightly toward him, but, of course, it was in his interest for her to be the rightful wife of Edward IV and their daughter to be a legitimate princess.

Elizabeth murmured a polite response and held her head submissively tilted. She refused to look at Margaret, for she could not bear to see the younger woman so satisfied with her victory.

This is for Bess. She reminded herself again and again as Margaret gushed over Henry's rise and plans for the kingdom's future.

Thankfully, the girl soon arrived, and Elizabeth found her part much easier to play in her presence. She placed a soft kiss on her daughter's cheek and ignored her surprise at her presence.

"Your betrothed is anxious to meet you," she said in false joy, hating the sing-song tone she heard in her own voice.

Bess looked doubtfully at her mother's hand as she attempted to drag her across the hall. "So, he is still my betrothed?"

Elizabeth had to close her eyes for a moment to gain the strength she needed to bear doubt from Bess along with Margaret's gloating. She made an encouraging reply, but found it wanting. Pausing amidst the many others eager to pay homage to the new king, she faced her daughter and gripped her passionately by the shoulders.

"You will be queen. Do not ever doubt it," she whispered intensely. They must both believe it. Otherwise, what had it all been for?

Peering into her mother's eyes as if trying to discern what motives hid behind them, Bess replied, "I do not doubt it."

Elizabeth released her before her emotions grew beyond her control. Resuming her path toward Tudor, she added, "He needs you. He knows as well as the rest of England that he has less than a drop of royal blood. He needs yours."

She hated herself for saying it. Hated making her daughter nothing more than a prized brood mare, but there was nothing else left.

"There he is."

She watched Bess quietly examine the man who would soon become her husband, and hoped that she sensed none of her mother's doubt. Henry had approached them, so Elizabeth presented her daughter and fell into another curtsey. Bess would take it from here. She should have no trouble charming the weary Lancastrian exile made king.

The softening of Henry's face as he spoke with Bess was obvious from across the room, and it made the grip of terror loosen on Elizabeth's heart. Maybe, just maybe, things could turn out alright for those loved ones she had remaining, thanks to the quiet strength of her eldest daughter.

March 1486

Cheyneygates was somehow soothing to Elizabeth now that she was not forced to be there. Her daughters had been surprised by her choice to lease the abbot's house now that it was not required for sanctuary. Elizabeth was somewhat surprised herself, for though the estate was more than adequate for her needs and in close proximity to Bess, it did not hold happy memories for her.

Maybe, she thought to herself but would never confess aloud, she felt that she recaptured that hopeful feeling that Edward would return when she was in this place. He had ridden in over a decade ago, just like a hero in a romance, and she could not help allowing a small portion of her heart to hope that he could do it again.

"How foolish I am," she muttered to herself.

Little Bridget glanced up at her mother's voice but somehow realized that the words were not meant for her, so she returned her attention to her dolls. The girl would never remember her father. Elizabeth was shocked by the revelation. A king, but not powerful enough to etch his essence into the memory of his youngest daughter, who had been little more than an infant when he died.

How long until Bess welcomed her first child into the world? She and Henry had been married in great ceremony two months earlier, and Elizabeth found that she was gladdened by the sincere feelings that the two seemed to share. Maybe this really was God's will, as Bess constantly claimed. She, of course, did not realize that it had all been carefully plotted out with little thought toward the ruler of heaven and earth.

Bess would call upon her when she was needed, Elizabeth was sure. Until then, it better suited her to not have the daily reminders of all that she had lost. Here at Cheyneygates, she could pretend that some of it might return.

April 1486

The man who stood before her could have been a ghost. His chestnut hair was longer and more disheveled than the last time she had seen him, and his face had aged years rather than months. However, Francis Lovell carried an aura of hope with him that lured Elizabeth into his presence like a moth to a flame.

"What are you doing here?" she demanded, intending to sound imperious but clearly announcing her eagerness to hear him out.

Francis had managed to make his way to her by pretending to be a messenger, but Elizabeth had recognized the good friend of King Richard immediately. What she could not fathom was what he was doing here, kneeling before her.

"Your grace," he began in a deep, confident voice. "I have come to ask for your favor."

Even her years of practice could not keep the shock from Elizabeth's face. Richard had held little love for her and his friends even less so. "Whatever do you mean?" she asked, searching his face for duplicity.

He surprised her further by taking up her hands in his. A fleeting thought raced through her mind that it had been so long since a man had touched her, but the intensity of his eyes kept her in the present.

"We need your support," he explained, squeezing her fingers almost painfully. "There is much you do not know."

Elizabeth laughed joylessly. "That we can easily agree upon."

She pulled her fingers from his grasp. The young man made her uncomfortable with his energetic presence and higher knowledge. Turning away, she casually asked, "What could you possibly have to tell me. My daughter is queen, and I am nobody. I have nothing left to me but living out my days praying that she bears the Tudor king a healthy heir."

"Your son is alive."

He had stated it quickly and purposefully. They may not know each other well, but Lovell understood that it was best to get straight to the point and let Elizabeth Woodville know what she had to gain before begging for her support.

Her steps halted, as did her heart. She did not turn back to him right away because she was attempting to make sense of the conflicting information racing through her brain.

With her back still to him, she whispered, "My son is alive?"

A part of her mind wondered which one. Edward? He had been raised to be king and would be almost old enough to try stealing back his crown. Richard? He had still been a playful, impetuous youth when she had been convinced to turn him over to the king's guards. Where could they have been all this time?

"My only remaining son serves his king and sister at the court of Henry VII," she stated firmly. She could not put Thomas in danger. This was a fantasy.

"No, you do not understand," Francis insisted, taking a step toward her as though he would touch her again. She moved away.

"Do you believe that I would have seen Tudor crowned if I believed one of Edward's sons survived?" Her voice was flat, unconcerned. She could not allow this dream to infect her reality.

"I do not believe you would have, your grace, no."

She examined him, one of Richard's best friends. Richard, who had supposedly had her sons killed. That was what everyone believed. Everyone, apparently, excepting the two people in this room.

"If you are trying to clear Richard's name," she began in a bored tone, "there is no need. I do not blame him for the murder of my sons."

Lovell appeared impressed but not shocked. Elizabeth allowed herself a small smile. She was better informed than he believed.

"Then you know he had them sent away to safety," he said eagerly, believing he had found the conspirator he sought.

Elizabeth sighed. This again. She could not bear to hear the litany that her daughters had preached to her for months repeated by this sycophant of her brother-in-law.

"Truly!" he insisted, seeing her doubt. "The plan was to send them both away," he began, letting some small amount of dejection to creep into his voice, "but at least Richard has made it safely to the court of Margaret in Burgundy."

Everything seemed to go black, and Elizabeth felt herself falling. Richard alive? Images of the boy with strawberry blond hair seared through her mind, more real than the scene before her. His laugh had been infectious, like his father's. Could he really be safe and sound with his aunt across the dark waters of the sea?

Her surroundings began to come back to her and Elizabeth realized she was upon a small couch with Francis Lovell's strong arm around her. She shoved him away.

"Accept my apology," he begged with his head hung contritely. "I should have asked you to sit before I spoke."

"Is it true?" she cried. "If it is not – if there is any chance that it is not – please do not mislead me! I could not bear it."

Hot tears burned her eyes, but she did not bother to brush them away. If her boy, Richard, was alive, nothing was as it should be.

"By God, it is!" Francis asserted. He grasped her hands again, and she did not pull away. "It is best that Tudor not realize the truth yet, but Richard's support is growing. He will be king."

A sob, or was it joyful laughter, escaped Elizabeth's body, and she embraced Francis as she would Richard were he there. He could not discern her mumbling as she clung to him, but he was sure he heard her cry, "My boy, my precious boy."

It was not until much later, after Francis had left with a bag heavy with gold committed to his cause, that Elizabeth paused to consider.

What would this mean for Bess?

September 1486

The fire crackled cheerily, and the wine was sweet and spiced. Elizabeth sat sipping the soothing liquid and staring into the flames, her emotions at war within her.

She had just assisted in her daughter's labor. A prince had been born.

Tumbled together in her overtaxed mind were images of her Richard, still at the court of Margaret of Burgundy, and her Bess, proudly cradling the baby she believed to be England's next king. Was God playing games with them?

Henry had ended the ongoing wars, and God had give him a son, but his head was not truly worthy of the crown. Was it?

Elizabeth closed her eyes and groaned. It would take all her strength, more than she believed she had available to call upon. When Richard returned, Bess would have to be content with being the king's sister.

Little Arthur. If he survived, he would be given appropriate titles by his uncle, and the dream of a King Arthur would remain just that.

And Henry? Elizabeth could admit that she had grown to respect him more than she anticipated. England was at peace and Bess was in love. But none of that would matter. Henry would be executed for treason when the true king returned.

June 1487

As Elizabeth crept through London alleys, she wondered where it would all lead. The stench that surrounded her made her feel secure. No one would expect to find the dowager queen amid the detritus and rodents, so she could move silently and secretly through the city in her peasant garb.

Flowing gowns were part of a past life. Her daily routine at Cheyneygates demanded a more subdued outfit. She was almost indifferentiable from the nuns. How Edward would laugh to see her! Many of her dresses and jewels had been discreetly sold so that she could send the money to Margaret in Burgundy to support Richard's household.

Elizabeth remained only partly convinced that Richard was alive, but she was willing to gamble on him. What else would she do with the painful reminders of her former position? Best that the resources she had be used to give her a tiny spark of hope.

It had almost flickered out. The rebellion, intended to call York to arms, had failed. Elizabeth prayed that Lovell still lived, but the news that had reached her was disheartening. The Yorkists gathered at Stoke had been as easily scattered before Tudor's troops as the rats that scampered away from her approach through the dismal corridor.

Elizabeth fumed as she stumbled over debris that she cared not to identify. She had warned them of the importance of a strong and confident stance. Surely, if there had not been such confusion over who they were fighting for, victory could have been theirs.

Sunlight struck Elizabeth's face as she exited the alley and found herself at the edge of a clean street lined with neat stalls and ladies shopping. It was eerily like entering another world. Had she not witnessed dogs fighting over a carcass just a few steps before? She had never realized just how close the dark things of this world were to the light.

Blinking to allow her eyes to adjust to the brightness, she searched for signs of the approaching caravan. They would come this way. She had seen it done before.

Her head was bowed to hide her face, but she still saw the bemused glances of children who wondered at her purpose. Assuming that merchants and shoppers must be looking at her the same way, Elizabeth attempted to move with purpose toward a stall. She bought a steaming meat pie to blend in with the crowd, but soon gave it to a pair of children who stared at her with their hunger shining in their eyes.

The sound of marching footsteps made Elizabeth's stomach turn far too much to consider eating it anyway. The prisoners had arrived.

The crowd scattered before horses and men proudly wearing the king's green and white livery. Following the men who had won the day, came those they had taken captive. Elizabeth moved with the rest of the women, who clutched children to their side and did not have to hide their faces as their eyes widened at the appearance of men in bloody bandages and worn clothing.

Elizabeth watched, praying that no one would recognize her. These men had fought for her son, though some of them did not know it. The boy among them had been called Edward of Warwick and Richard of York. That had been their mistake, Elizabeth was sure.

She had agreed that Richard should not be part of the fighting. He was too young. Too precious. Using another boy in his place made sense until their victory was certain. However, claiming the pretender to be Warwick was too easily disproven. Everyone knew Henry had the real York prince locked up in the Tower.

How could they have been so stupid?

Elizabeth pressed her lips into a thin line as she scanned the prisoners faces for the countenances of John de la Pole and Francis

Lovell. Maybe she should have allowed Richard to be present. As young as he was, he had a charismatic presence like his father that could have ensured their victory.

Or he could have died. No, it was better this way. Richard could fight another day.

The procession had almost passed, and Elizabeth had spotted neither of the leading Yorkist men among them. Before anyone could recognize her, she turned back to the alley that had brought her here.

As she traipsed her way through the dark, dank passageway, she prayed that they had survived.

~ ~ ~ ~

"How could he?" Bess cried.

Elizabeth held her but said nothing. The news that John de la Pole had been killed in the Battle of Stoke crushed them both, but not for the same reasons.

"He had reconciled with Henry," Bess continued through her sobbing. "He had never pressed his claim as Richard's heir."

"No, he had not," Elizabeth agreed noncommittally. "Of course, he was not doing that now either."

She had been surprised to be called to her daughter's side, but now she understood. Bess needed to grieve for her York cousin before receiving Henry. He returned victorious over rebels and would not wish to comfort a disappointed wife.

"You do not truly believe he was fighting for that boy, do you?" Bess asked through her sniffling. "They could not even agree on who he was."

Biting her tongue, Elizabeth weighed her response. "He must have believed in what he was fighting for."

"That is just what I do not understand!" Bess cried. "What was he fighting for? For Edward, who is in the Tower and has no desire to be king? For himself? Then why did he not simply say so?

Why did he hold up this pretender instead of remaining loyal to my son?"

Elizabeth sighed. To Bess, this was about Arthur. She could not accept that, to other men, the fight was still about York versus Henry. Arthur was too young for their loyalty.

"Henry has won the day for Arthur," she reminded her daughter, though she had to force the words around the lump in her throat. John's death had been a huge blow to the cause, and she had yet to hear from Francis. She prayed Richard would have those men he needed to claim his crown when the time came.

Bess continued to cry, and Elizabeth simply held her. There was nothing more for either of them to say.

Elizabeth was surprised when Bess came to her again the following day. Composed now, the tears and feelings of betrayal were left behind, and she held herself with the dignity of the queen she was. Elizabeth's smile faded before it could fully form as she examined her daughter's face.

She knew. But how much?

"Henry has decided that it is time for you to retire to Bermondsey Abbey."

Bess did not greet her mother or move to embrace her. The lines had been drawn, and she took the side of her husband and son. How ironic, Elizabeth thought, that she had practically forced her daughter to marry Henry and now the girl clung to him as her savior.

Elizabeth opened her mouth to speak before changing her mind and clamping it shut. They do not know all, she decided. Henry knew that she was involved in some way and wanted her gone, but he does not know about Richard. If he did, he would not simply be forcing her to retire to a nunnery.

Steeling her spine, Elizabeth nodded her acceptance of the punishment. She would say nothing that might give them a clue of

Richard's existence. She would sacrifice herself for him.

"I will pack my things now."

"Good," Bess said, but the word was almost a sob. Taking a deep breath, she attempted to speak again. "Mother, how could you?" But this inquiry trailed off into tears once again. As Elizabeth searched for what she could offer that would not harm Richard, Bess held up a hand.

No, she did not want to hear her mother's excuses.

"God go with you," Bess whispered before turning away. On her way out, she nodded toward the men who had been instructed to see that the dowager queen was moved to more secure quarters before the end of the day.

November 1487

From her small room at Bermondsey, Elizabeth heard of her daughter's coronation. Tudor had taken his time and made certain he had an heir first, but he had finally made his York bride a queen. The news made Elizabeth wonder if she was doing the right thing. Should she be content with her daughter on the throne or hope in the promise that her son still lived?

Every time she convinced herself to give up her dream and support Bess, the image of a young man with a crown atop his red-gold head would dissuade her. Richard should be king. Not Henry, whose mother thought she had done the murderous work to clear the way for him.

It always came down to that. She loved her sweet Bess, but it was Henry who ruled.

June 1488

The days at Bermondsey flowed together into a calm routine that Elizabeth found herself remarkably soothed by. While it might not have been her choice to reside there, she found that she was glad that she did. Her room was small and immaculately clean. The walls were made up of tiny, pale bricks that seemed to hold the secrets of the room's past residents.

Through her window, Elizabeth could watch life that she used to participate in pass by, and she found that she did not miss much of it. She enjoyed observing the barges on the Thames and merchants in the square, but, for the first time in her life, was content to fill her time with prayer and contemplation.

That was good because life had left her little else.

Still uncertain about the survival of her son, Richard, and not at liberty to investigate the matter, Elizabeth finally found the solace in her devotions that she had formerly only heard others speak of. She had always been a woman of action, for better or for worse. Now, the decisions and actions must be left to others.

A warm breeze brought in the fragrance of flowers along with the murky scent of the river, and Elizabeth closed her eyes to bask in the scents and sounds that surrounded her but demanded nothing from her. She was surprised by a knock at her door bringing her back to the present.

The timid girl who brought Elizabeth's meals each day peeked in to announce a visitor. One of her daughters, Elizabeth guessed, for there were no other visitors to the dowager queen. Joy rose in Elizabeth's chest as she wondered which it would be. Cecily, most likely, and hopefully she would have Bridget in tow. A visit from the outspoken young woman and bright child would bring great cheer to their mother.

Elizabeth did not expect the woman who stepped in, but she quickly fell into a curtsey before her. Bess, now queen and mother of the heir to the kingdom, lay a pale hand upon her mother's head and said, "Bless you, mother. Please rise. It is not necessary for you to honor me this way."

Rising, Elizabeth did not give voice to her inner turmoil and fear that she owed her daughter much more. The peace that Bermondsey gave her flew away in the presence of the daughter she had controlled and betrayed. Instead of the happiness the visit should have given her, fear gripped her. What plans did the king have for her now?

Bess seemed to be taking in the room. Was she comparing it to the luxurious queen's quarters that Elizabeth had formerly claimed? After a moment, her eyes sought her mother's.

"Are you well?" she asked, the question carrying many more inquiries than an observer might realize.

Elizabeth nodded, remembering the tranquility she had felt only moments before, "Surprisingly so," she admitted. "I am content here."

The small smile Bess allowed gave Elizabeth a warm sensation. She knew without asking that her daughter had forgiven her.

"I have come with news," Bess continued in a more formal manner. She moved toward her mother, but the room seemed too small for her elaborate skirts.

Elizabeth's heart sank. The only news pertaining to her would involve King James of Scotland. Henry had taken it into his mind to betroth the dowager queen to him in an attempt to secure peace. And to be rid of her, Elizabeth had no doubt. However, she could not imagine living in Scotland or being queen to anyone but her Edward. She had told Bess as much, but Henry had proven time and again that he would not be ruled by his wife.

Before Elizabeth could form an objection to what she was certain her daughter was going to say, Bess spoke, "King James has been killed."

She did not say more. They both understood that few would mourn the ineffective, unpopular king.

Elizabeth tried not to look too grateful and muttered, "God rest his soul."

"He was killed in a battle with his own nobles who held his son up to replace him," Bess added, narrowing her eyes at her mother.

Pressing her lips together, Elizabeth did not reply. She deserved that, she supposed.

Bess dropped her gaze and fidgeted with the rings that sparkled on her small fingers. She seemed to regret the attack if her mother would not rise to it. Taking a deep breath, she began again, "You are sure you have all you need?"

Elizabeth opened her arms to the cozy space. "The only thing that could please me more is frequent visits from my daughters."

Bess smiled and gestured to the window. "Shall we walk in the gardens?"

With a nod, Elizabeth stepped to her daughter's side. "Yes, I would like that."

The afternoon had been idyllic, Elizabeth reflected later. The sun had set, and a single candle gave weak light to the room. She was preparing to extinguish it and go to bed when another knock sounded at her door.

Confusion furrowed her brow as Elizabeth moved to open it. The same timid servant stood on the other side, this time holding out a tightly folded square of parchment. The girl said nothing but offered a quick curtsey and left the missive with Elizabeth.

Before closing the door, Elizabeth scanned the hall for any observers. It was an unspoken rule that she did not receive communication that was not first read by the prioress, but this note had a clearly unbroken seal. Who could it be from?

Her fingers fumbled at the seal in her eagerness. The note was grimy and wrinkled as though it had traveled far in secret places. Her eyes found the end of the letter first.

Francis Lovell.

Most thought he had died in the Battle of Stoke alongside John de la Pole, but there was his name bold as could be. Elizabeth's eyes flew to the top of the page.

He had escaped to Burgundy where he was working with Margaret to prepare Richard for making his claim. A tingling sensation ran up and down Elizabeth's spine as it did whenever she allowed herself to believe that her son was alive.

Then she remembered her afternoon with Bess, who was England's queen. Elizabeth shook her head and read the note again, more slowly and carefully this time.

As she did so, doubt began to creep into her heart. Without being able to place her finger on exactly what was wrong, Elizabeth began to wonder about some of the phrases Francis employed in the letter.

He asked for funds, which was to be expected, but he also spoke of Richard's training. Elizabeth wondered what that could be beyond the military skills he would require. Whatever did Francis mean when he said Richard was being prepared for court? He had lived at court most of his life, but maybe his Aunt Margaret found something in him lacking.

Laying down the note, Elizabeth peered into the darkness and wondered. She was not as impetuous as she once was about scheming, not since it had led to her daughter marrying Tudor. However, if there was any chance for Richard, she must support him. With a sigh, she wondered how she would arrange for a letter and gold to be delivered to Burgundy.

November 1489

Elizabeth had been thrilled when Bess requested that she attend her in the birth of her second child. Whatever had passed between them, this was a moment that a daughter wanted her mother. The bad feelings that Elizabeth thought might assail her upon reentering the palace she used to call her own never came. She truly had made peace with her lot.

Except for when the infrequent communications from Burgundy reached her.

However, she would not think of the possibility that her youngest son was across the sea hoping to reclaim his kingdom. Not today.

The pains had begun, and Elizabeth focused her efforts on distracting her daughter from the feeling that she was being torn in two. She knew that nothing she said made a difference to the sweating, panting woman before her, yet she continued to remind her that she was a queen, and even more a York, and she would birth this babe.

She noticed that Bess was staring at a tapestry of the angel chorus as they brought news of the Christ child to the shepherds. Even Mary, mother of God, had been forced to share this trial. Elizabeth fleetingly wondered how a woman could be so devoted to a God who put her in such a position.

The hours passed with soothing words, quiet prayers, and cool cloths for the queen's forehead. Elizabeth was weary. She straightened from her stoop at the bedside and was shocked by the pain that racked her own body and almost undeniable urge to lie down and rest right there on the floor.

"Mother!" Bess screamed, drawing her away from her own concerns. "It is happening too quickly!" her terrified daughter cried.

Elizabeth returned to her post with words of comfort and

even prayed with Bess between the pains and found that she was calmed by it. The midwife treated Elizabeth like one more lady-in-waiting rather than a former queen, but she found it surprisingly refreshing and laughed aloud at her stern manner. Soon, the terror that Bess had expressed proved unnecessary.

A perfectly formed child was placed in her arms – perfect except for the fact that it had been born a girl.

This, of course, did not disappoint Elizabeth one iota, and she hoped that Henry would be kindhearted about it. Poor Arthur would have to wait for a brother to cross swords with.

Elizabeth did not wait to discover Henry's reaction to his daughter. Once she was assured that Bess was recovering normally, Elizabeth took a barge to Bermondsey. As the cold wind snapped through the tent she took refuge in onboard, she huddled into her fur cloak and eagerly anticipated her bed. She was abnormally sore and weary from the episode but wrote it off to old age with a sigh.

November 1491

Richard IV.

The people of Ireland had received her son as king. The news had reached her, and now she must deal with its consequences. Elizabeth peered around her tidy, little room. So much less than she had become accustomed to. So much more than many had.

Would Henry leave her with less? Would he imprison her in the Tower as he had Edward of Warwick?

Elizabeth gulped down the terror that threatened to rise in her throat.

"Let him do his worst," she announced to the empty room, lifting her chin as if a crown still rested upon her head.

She had sacrificed so much for her children. If only it had not set them against one another, but Bess would have to be content with her reduced position when Richard took his crown. Surely, she would see that it was his by right.

A familiar pain shot through Elizabeth's thin chest, and she knew that it would not be long before her children could no longer blame her for their positions in life. She had done all she could to seek advantages for them, but God would soon set her upon a new journey.

The view from her window was of autumn leaves and fisherman in hats and scarves. Summer flowers had all faded, and she knew that she would not see them again. Elizabeth was not afraid. She may not share the submissive piety of her daughter, but she was confident in God's presence and felt that he would find a place for her in the next world. A place next to Edward. It was where she belonged.

February 1492

The girl whose name Elizabeth could never remember set a tray near the bed and sat upon a stool to tempt her with bites of food. As she turned her head away from most of the offerings, Elizabeth felt a blanket of guilt weigh down on her. The nameless girl had clearly taken risks for her, allowing secret communications and serving Elizabeth well. However, she could not bring herself to finish a meal for her.

The pain was no longer searing and infrequent, but a constant dull ache that never left. It had become akin to an old friend, holding Elizabeth's hand and beckoning her toward a new adventure. When the sweet liquid the girl poured down her throat lessened it for a few hours, Elizabeth almost missed it.

Elizabeth forced herself to focus her cloudy vision upon the girl. She was pretty in a plain sort of way, the kind of girl who would be beautiful to her husband but unnoteworthy to others. Elizabeth was suddenly reminded of Emma, a lady-in-waiting who had served Bess but had died of the sweating sickness. Now why on earth was she thinking of her?

"Why do you serve me so kindly?" Elizabeth whispered while avoiding another bite of pottage.

The girl dipped her head in an attempt to hide her blush. "You are a queen, your grace," she said, her awe of her patient clear in the whispered words.

Elizabeth closed her eyes. It had been so long since someone had called her 'your grace.' An image of Edward formed behind her lids. Not heavy and wasted by drink as he had become, but muscular and vigorous as he had been when they first married. The golden crown had shimmered upon his head, but she would have wanted him just the same had it been a fisherman's cap.

"Please, try a bit more," the girl begged, breaking into Elizabeth's daydream.

She did not wish to eat more. She did not want her life lengthened. Edward beckoned.

Time must have passed, because the tray had been removed and the girl stood near the door as though she had just entered the room.

"Your daughters are here, your grace," she said in a voice just above a whisper as if full volume would somehow hurt the invalid. "The queen and her sisters," she clarified.

"Help me dress," Elizabeth insisted. She would not receive her daughters abed like an old woman.

Her eyes widened, but the girl hurried to assist Elizabeth. Little choice she had as the dowager queen had already tossed her covers clumsily aside and would somehow stand, with or without her.

It exhausted Elizabeth to change into the simple linen dress that had become too large for her, but she stood to receive her daughters, careful to keep her hand from pressing her breast where the pain was worst.

"You have even brought my little Cat!" she exclaimed as the pretty twelve-year-old skipped into the room.

Bess and Anne followed close behind, but Elizabeth wished Bridget was with them. Her youngest had already been devoted to the church and resided at Dartford.

"Do you know that they believe our brother, Richard, has landed in Ireland to reclaim his crown?" Catherine exclaimed, proud to prove she knew the latest court gossip.

The room fell silent for only a moment before Elizabeth said the only thing she could say, "Likely only fools believe that." Acting as though the thought of her son regaining his kingdom was no more noteworthy than the arrival of a troop of performers, Elizabeth quickly changed the subject, "I hear that you are expecting another child," she directed toward Bess.

Cat's face fell. She had been certain that her mother would rejoice in the news of their brother Richard, but she and Bess had simply moved on to discussing babies. Her mother gave Bess a cryptic warning about not wishing for too many sons that made little sense to Cat, for even she knew that it was a wife's duty to produce many sons.

Elizabeth asked Anne about Cecily's new daughter to coax the quiet girl into the conversation. Henry needed to marry the timid girl to a man who could draw her out of her shell, she thought. When Anne made a wistful comment about Viscount Welles and his attentiveness to Cecily, Elizabeth wished that it were still within her power to select a husband for her.

Bess was also smiling at the dreamy-eyed girl, and Elizabeth nodded, satisfied. Her queen would see to her future when her mother could not.

It was challenging for all of them to keep the discussion on trivial matters of daily life when there was so much more going on in the larger world. Bess could not ask her mother if she knew that faithful Yorkists had traveled to France to see for themselves this man who called himself Richard IV. Elizabeth could not ask her daughter if Henry truly believed him to be the York heir. As they discussed needlework and the coming of spring, their more important questions were withheld.

Elizabeth thought she should be applauded for her efforts at hiding her weariness until Bess announced, "We must allow you to rest, mother."

It could not have been more than an hour, but Elizabeth's shoulders slumped now that there was no reason to keep up the façade. She did need to rest, as much as she did not wish for her daughters to leave. Who knew when she would see them again.

"Your mother is an old woman," she admitted with a combination of sadness and frustration welling in her eyes.

She could not hold the tears back when Bess whispered, "I love you, mother," as she embraced her.

Her response seemed inadequate, words of pride and praise that allowed her to swipe away her tears and lighten the moment. Bess would be a better queen than she had been....until Richard returned.

Elizabeth held each girl longer than she had since they were small and tried to affix the feeling into her memory to be called up during her long, lonely hours. To transition from a palace and a large, bustling family to a quiet, solitary room was sometimes a blessing, sometimes a burden.

A few moments after they had filed from the room, Elizabeth watched them climb onto their barge. They did not look up. Maybe none of them had realized that Elizabeth's window view would include them. She did not mind. Somehow it made their gestures and grins more authentic since they did not know their mother observed them.

Forcing her strength to last long enough to watch her daughters' barge disappear down the river, Elizabeth finally collapsed into bed and was almost instantly asleep. In her dreams, she was young, Edward was alive, and their future still seemed golden before them.

June 1492

A warm, soothing breeze caressed Elizabeth's skin. It made her think of strolling through summer gardens and secret afternoons stolen with Edward when he should have been seeing to the needs of the kingdom. His image was so vivid before her that she had to remind herself that her eyes were closed. He was not lying next to her in this narrow priory bed.

No one was with her. Bess had entered her confinement chamber with Cecily and Anne attending her. That was as it should be. Better that they attend a birth than a death.

It was approaching. Elizabeth could feel it, but she was not afraid. On the contrary, she was ready to welcome it. She no longer belonged here.

The only time the will to live surged through her was when she considered Richard. How she wished to see this man who claimed to be her son. She would know for certain if it was him, regardless of the time that had passed. A woman knows the children of her womb just as God knows each of his.

God was not going to give her that desire, and she had to be content to leave it to Bess. When Richard invaded, would Bess recognize him? If she did, would she step down to support him as king? Surely, she would. Bess was a woman who prided herself on doing the right thing. She would not be able to live with herself knowing she had rejected the rightful king – and her brother no less.

Yes, Elizabeth could be secure in leaving it to Bess.

It was not precisely true that no one was with her. The girl, whose name still escaped her cloudy mind, was there. She patiently cajoled Elizabeth into taking a few bites here a few sips there. It was not enough to sustain her, but it no longer mattered.

Elizabeth knew that she should thank the girl for her care and the risks that she had taken for her, but her eyes would not open and her voice would not rise. Another task to be left to Bess. The largess of the queen would be a great reward for the nameless girl.

The image of Edward came to her again, and every part of her ached to join him. The summer scented breeze disheveled his copper colored hair, and his smile was as disarming as ever. She knew every inch of his tall, strong body and longed to touch him again. If only her own body were not old and frail. It had become a prison where it had once brought her such pleasure.

He reached out to her, and she willed her limbs to move toward him. Elizabeth was frustrated with the separation. It had gone on too long. Edward's teasing made her struggle anew to open her eyes and accept her reality as inadequate as it was.

However, she was surprised to see that her hand did reach out to him this time. His hand was warm and rough, just as it had always been. Years of battle had left his palms permanently callused by the pommel of his sword. Hers was soft and smooth as a girl's.

Elizabeth felt herself pulled toward him but was worried that she would not be able to stand. She had grown so weak.

She need not have worried. Her weariness and pain fell away as though she were a butterfly leaving its cocoon, and she went to him.

The cries of the girl who had devotedly served her queen went unheard. Elizabeth's daughters would mourn once the news reached them, but there were few others who remained to cry for Elizabeth Woodville. She was an unpleasant reminder of another time when cousin fought cousin and the crown rested uneasily on one head then another.

Elizabeth was gone along with the Plantagenet dream that had truly died with her husband.

It was up to Bess now. The Tudor dynasty had begun.

Afterword

Elizabeth of York (Bess), gave birth to a daughter on July 2, 1492. The baby was named Elizabeth in honor of her recently deceased grandmother.

The man who called himself Richard IV has gone down in history as Perkin Warbeck. Was he a pretender from Tournai or a royal Plantagenet prince? He was recognized by various European leaders as England's king, but was that because they believed him or because they wanted to expose Henry's weaknesses?

In 1495, this man made his first unsuccessful attempt to invade England but ended up in Scotland where he was recognized as Richard IV by James IV. Lady Catherine Gordon was wed to him in 1496, believing she would reign as queen. Another invasion was attempted in 1497, and the would-be king was captured.

On November 23, 1499, the man called Perkin Warbeck was hanged at Tyburn for treason.

Additional Reading

For those interested in reading more about the historical figures featured in this novel, I recommend the following sources:

Elizabeth of York: The Forgotten Tudor Queen by Amy Licence

Winter King: Henry VII and the Dawn of Tudor England by Thomas Penn

The Perfect Prince: The Mystery of Perkin Warbeck and His Quest for the Throne of England by Ann Wroe

The Woodvilles: The Wars of the Roses and England's Most Infamous Family by Susan Higginbotham

Author's Note

Elizabeth Woodville is a historical figure that I have had some trouble connecting with. Unlike the other women I have written about, she seemed less pure, more motivated by self-interest. However, after spending more time with her I can sympathize with her almost impossible situation.

With her husband and protector dead, what was an unpopular queen to do? I believe she did try to do her best, and not only for herself but for her remaining children.

Did Elizabeth plot with pretenders or believe that Lambert Simnel or Perkin Warbeck could have been her son? I do not know, but I cannot imagine her trying to guess and decide whether to give them her support or be content that her daughter was the mother of the new dynasty.

Elizabeth Woodville is often judged harshly, but few of us have had to cope with the hardships life dealt her. Like anyone else, she had strengths and weaknesses. She could be kind and generous, but she could also be self-serving. Elizabeth reached very high for herself and her children, and it is undeniable that she left her mark on history.

This story coincides with the story of Elizabeth of York told in *Plantagenet Princess, Tudor Queen*, where you may continue to read about the fate of Bess and the remainder of the York remnant.

Samantha Wilcoxson

Prince of York

A Story of Reginald Pole

Samantha Wilcoxson

'Until now I had thought God had given me the grace of being the son of one of the best and most honoured ladies in England, and I gloried in it, thanks to his Divine Majesty; but now he has vouchsafed to honour me still more, by making me the son of a martyr.'
- Cardinal Reginald Pole upon hearing of his mother's execution

'Believe as firmly as if your salvation depended upon faith alone; act as if good works were all sufficient.'
- Cardinal Reginald Pole on justification

August 1541

Was God within the cold stones of the cathedral floor?

Reginald wondered as he lay still, prostrated upon the unforgiving surface, his arms outstretched as if nailed to an invisible cross. He thanked God for the aches the position caused, for he had much to make restitution for. Could God forgive a man who had caused the death of his mother?

Uncharacteristic guilt washed over him like crashing waves as he considered the fact that he had successfully evaded the assassins of King Henry of England never foreseeing that the petulant monarch would turn on his family to complete his revenge.

"I spoke only the truth, Lord," he whispered. His beard faintly scratched against the stone and his breath was stale in his nostrils. "I seek only to do your will. Reveal it to me," he begged with his eyes squeezed shut though it was dark beneath his blood-red robes.

After a few moments of listening intently to the silence for God's message hidden there, Reginald heard footsteps. He sighed, leaving a film of condensation upon the floor.

As he drew in his arms to stand, Reginald forced away thoughts of his older brothers, Henry and Arthur. They enjoyed the peace and comfort of heaven as well as the company of their mother now.

He did not hesitate to leave Alvise waiting, for that was certainly who it must be disturbing the peace of the cathedral. He first rose only as far as his knees, pausing there to offer a prayer of thanksgiving. He must not only mourn but remember the blessings God continuously gave him. Then Reginald moved to his feet in one practiced, fluid motion. He bowed low before the altar before finally turning to his dear friend.

Although the men were of a similar age, Alvise carried his

years more lightly. His face was round and open where Reginald's was stern and rather narrow. Alvise's bright eyes always examined the world with curious enthusiasm and looked up to Reginald much as a mentor as a friend. The lines around his eyes attested that Reginald could spend endless hours studying, while Alvise had an impetuous spirit that made it impossible for him to be still for long. They complemented each other well, their differences bringing them closer instead of causing conflict.

"You are recalled to Rome!" Alvise exclaimed.

For Alvise, Rome held promises of excitement and adventure, palaces and feasts. Therefore, he was surprised when Reginald's shoulders drooped and face fell at the news. A very different vision of Rome filled Reginald's mind. When he was last in the city, the Pope had provided him with a bodyguard to avoid King Henry's assassins. The corruption and chaos of the city invaded the heart and mind, and Reginald had little desire to return.

"There is a messenger," Alvise explained, some of the anticipation draining from his voice.

Reginald was already moving toward the door, having assumed an envoy must have leaked a portion of his mission to Alvise upon arrival. It was his duty to receive the remainder of the command, little as he would like it.

As he strolled through the narrow streets of Capranica, an ancient village tucked into the hills surrounding Rome, Reginald could not help but compare the beauty and serenity of his surroundings with the bustling crowds of Rome. Here, Reginald could spend an afternoon studying by the shores of a lake that contained water so clear it could not even be called blue. In Rome, he would be forced to employ guards and stay off the streets as much as possible.

King Henry would have been informed that Reginald had

taken up residence in Capranica, but his spies and assassins could not reach him as easily where one who does not belong is quickly spotted.

Still, it was Reginald's duty to God and his church on earth to go where he was called. And so, he would go.

~ ~ ~ ~

The road to Rome was traveled in a single day, so Reginald's small entourage arrived almost before the messenger's return. Pietro Bembo was the first to greet him, and the elderly priest made Reginald feel as though he were being welcomed home by a kindly father.

"Ah, Reynaldo!" Cardinal Bembo cried in a voice gone soft with age and hours of rhetoric. He had never been able to form his tongue around the English 'Reginald' and preferred his Italian substitute. He embraced the younger man, the top of his grey head coming approximately to Reginald's shoulder.

"It does my heart good to see you," Bembo said, taking Reginald's arm and leading him through the wide halls of the Vatican.

Reginald's smile was genuine. If he must be in Rome, he would at least enjoy the company of his many good friends whom he had missed during his time away.

"You must share your latest verses with me," he said, trying to ignore the fact that the aging cardinal leaned into him to ease the pain in his joints.

"An evening of poetry! That is just what we shall have." Bembo patted Reginald on the arm as he planned the event aloud as they walked.

Eventually, Reginald decided to interrupt as Bembo was considering who to invite. "Do you know why I have been summoned?" Reginald asked. "It was the Holy Father who sent me away – for my own safety, of course. Why does he call me back?"

The patting on the arm increased in intensity as Bembo reassured him, "Oh, for a good reason. A very good reason indeed!"

Feeling some of his anxiety ease at Bembo's positive words, Reginald stood taller and happily bore the burden of the other man's weight until they reached the hall where he was to be received.

Although Reginald had known him when he was simply Alessandro Farnese, he was still in some awe when he approached the throne of Pope Paul III. He did not bow as low as he was able but matched his posture to Bembo's capabilities. Rising, Reginald addressed the man who had been his friend and mentor since he first came to Italy as a young man.

"Your Holiness," Reginald said, keeping his head tilted in reverence.

"Reginald! There is no need for formality in the presence of friends," Paul exclaimed as he left his gilded chair to greet them. The white of his fine clothing made a startling contrast with the red of the cardinals' robes. "How are you, my friend? Has dear Pietro here worn out your ears already?"

Bembo opened his mouth to protest, but Reginald was quicker. "There is no one else I would rather have welcome me back to Rome," Reginald insisted. The unspoken question hung in the air. Why was he here?

"I'll not leave you in suspense. You shall not have to stay long in Rome," Paul began with a sidelong grin that exposed more teeth missing than present. He did know Reginald well. "I asked you here because I have decided to name you as legate."

The Pope's chest puffed out visibly, even under the layers of fabric, so Reginald knew that this was to be an assignment he would welcome unlike some of the tasks he had undertaken for the sake of the church.

"Yes, Holy Father?" Reginald urged in the silence that Pope

Paul seemed to want him to fill.

His grin was broad as one who is imparting a generous gift. "I would like you to serve as my governor in Viterbo."

Reginald was known for being slow and deliberate in his speech, but this time he simply did not know what to say. It was an ideal assignment in the peaceful countryside.

"It's not too far from Rome," Paul was reminding him. "I need to have you close enough to take advantage of your council when I need it."

"Of course," Reginald murmured. He could not have chosen a better position for himself. "You honor me greatly, Your Holiness."

The honorific was already being waved away. "Nonsense. Few have done more or served God as loyally as you have. As your entire family has."

Silence fell and smiles faded as the three men considered all that Reginald had lost in his mission to bring the King of England to repentance. His older brother and mother executed. His young nephew still in the Tower. Because of Reginald's words.

No. He mentally chided himself. Because of King Henry's selfishness and desire to set himself up as a god. Thankfully, he was not left long with his thoughts.

"You will have your quiet peace, time to study, and important work to do," the Pope said, "and I will have you close enough at hand to please me."

"Thank you," Reginald said, taking the hand of the Holy Father in a firm grip between both of his own. They had been through much together and there was much that he could say, but he settled for, "Thank you, truly."

The assignment received, Reginald and Alvise were able to enjoy a few days in Rome. Taking comfort in the comradery of his friends and fellow cardinals, Reginald began to wonder what had made him dread the trip.

The evening that Bembo planned allowed Reginald to remember everything he had loved about Rome in the days before assassins hid in shadows and crowds held dangerous enemies. Cardinal Contarini handed him a glass of wine almost before he was fully inside the doorway.

"I have been anxious to see you again," Contarini said. The greeting was inane enough, but concern filled his eyes. The last time Reginald had seen him was when he received the news of his mother's execution.

"Thank you, Gasparo. You are a true friend." Reginald accepted the sympathy and the glass together. "Rather than mourn, I thank God for honoring my mother enough to make her a martyr to his cause. I only hope that one day I may do as much to bring glory to his name."

"Amen," Contarini murmured with a dip of his head.

"You must fill me in on the results of the conversations in Regensburg," Reginald insisted, changing the topic to one that was more palatable to him. "I understand that you were able to come to a surprising agreement on the matter of justification."

Contarini smiled but held up a hand to forestall undue praise. "The final document was agreed upon, yes, but it is vague enough that it does me little credit. In the end, I was unable to get Melanchton to budge on a variety of important matters."

"Yet what could be more vital than justification itself?" Reginald asked.

The point was conceded with a nod, though they both knew that authority of the pope and transubstantiation were no small matters, and it was these that remained stumbling blocks between the Church of Rome and the Protestants.

"I feel we may have had more success if you had been able to remain," Contarini said with a shrug, "but perhaps it would make no difference. You have a gift for seeing the world through eyes of others, but these Protestants are hard-headed and none more so than Luther himself."

"It is a profound philosophy, Gasparo. *Sola fide. Sola scriptura.* Luther is difficult to counter in his preaching of the authority of scripture. He is talented at making it sound as though each of his own words come from God himself."

"That is just it!" Contarini cried as he held out his glass to be refilled with Bembo's fine red wine. "He plays the humble monk while acting as though it is he that is God's representative on earth rather than the Holy Father."

"A fine trick, indeed," Reginald agreed thoughtfully. "Yet, does not Luther debate his fellow Protestants on the eucharist? It is not the Lutherans who deny the true presence in the bread and wine."

"The wine! Isn't it exquisite?" This exclamation came from just behind Reginald, and he turned to find Bembo tipping his glass to him. "I told you we would have a fine evening to welcome our Reynaldo back to Rome!"

Bembo shuffled forward as he gestured fondly toward the generous display of food and drink as well as the many men gathered to share in it.

"Yes, thank you, Pietro," Reginald said. "As Cicero tells us, there is nothing of greater value than true friendship."

"So, you have been working on your book," Bembo said, beaming up at Reginald like a proud tutor. "Wonderful!"

Only his close friends knew that Reginald enjoyed studying the work of the famous Roman orator for he feared his ability to ever complete his reflections upon it.

"Slowly," Reginald admitted. "I make my annotations only when I do not have more important duties. It shall be a project for my retirement."

"I do not see you as a man made for quiet retirement," Contarini interjected.

Bembo laughed, "No, not Reynaldo. He is too important to the church to be allowed to spend his days basking in the sun."

Reginald smiled and bowed his head in acceptance of the compliment, but he did wonder if he would ever finish his book on Cicero or at least not have to worry about outrunning assassins.

The rest of the evening passed pleasantly, and Reginald had little reason to remain in Rome afterward. As he had been the first to greet him, old Bembo was there to see him off as well.

"Come visit me in Viterbo, Pietro," Reginald said, grasping him fondly by the arms.

"Oh, not me," Bembo declined, shaking his head emphatically. "Even a day's ride is too much for me these days."

Reginald would have insisted, but he sensed the truth of his old friend's words. It saddened him to realize the extent of his physical decline. Pietro Bembo was the closest thing had to a father, his real father long dead and scarcely found in his memory.

"You will send me your verse," Reginald said instead.

"Yes, yes," Bembo agreed, now nodding enthusiastically. "And I would see your work on Cicero."

Reginald smiled and assured him that he would send it to him once he had completed something worth sharing.

"Your writing is much like his, you know," Bembo continued.

"You honor me too much," Reginald said, shaking his head at the very idea that his words might go down in history the way Cicero's had.

"Just you wait and see," Bembo murmured, patting him on the arm. "Just you wait and see."

October 1541

It was an ideal time of year for travel, and Reginald wondered if Pope Paul had considered that before giving him the assignment. Alvise had been surprisingly eager to leave Rome as well. He enjoyed the city but kept poorly hidden his fear for Reginald's safety. He shared Reginald's joy over the move to Viterbo and had extended many invitations to friends to visit them once they were resettled.

They had not ventured far from the city when two horsemen came into view. The strangers had dismounted and were examining the foreleg of one of their mounts. The horses were sleek and handsome, but their riders wore the ordinary clothing of servants. Reginald thought they must be on an errand for their master and would be worried about the consequences of laming one of his fine stallions.

Bringing their caravan to a halt, Reginald looked to Alvise, who was already leaping to the ground to see what could be done. As Reginald climbed down from his horse a bit more carefully than his companion, he could only hear the murmur of voices that held an overtone of concern. As he walked toward the small group, he realized they were speaking English and furrowed his brow.

"What appears to be the problem, Alvise? Can we help our unfortunate friends in any way?" he asked.

As Alvise offered a shrug and his opinion that the horse seemed well enough, one of the strangers stood from where he squatted at the horse's feet. He offered words of appreciation and introduction, but there was a gleam in his eyes that Reginald found disturbing.

"I am Edwin, and my friend here," the stranger gestured to his companion who remained kneeling near their horse, "is Roger."

"What is your errand?" Reginald asked. He forced his concerns to the back of his mind. He could not allow King Henry to make him afraid to help a person in need. It demonstrated a lack of faith to see danger around every corner.

"We have a delivery to make, but a scurrying rodent gave the horse a scare. I am afraid that in his panic he has injured the leg too much for riding," Edwin explained with more gesturing toward the poor horse and the small crowd gathered around Roger.

Reginald looked toward the men kneeling around the horse's leg but did not join them. He was certain he could add nothing to their examination.

"Perhaps I can offer you some refreshment while Alvise confers with Roger." Reginald turned to his saddlebags and retrieved a leather flask of watered wine and a few small apples. He offered one to Edwin and each man in his retinue as those who considered themselves more knowledgeable in such matters discussed the horse's ability to make it into the city.

"You are not far," Reginald added. "We have only left this morning." He turned to gesture behind them and peer at the skyline as if he might be able to make out Rome's tall stone buildings on the horizon, though hills and forest stood between them.

At the moment Reginald's back was turned, a furious scuffling broke out behind him. Rather than spinning around to defend himself, Reginald instinctively curled his body into a protective position. The sounds of quick footsteps were accompanied by a cloud of dust that swiftly enveloped the small group. Slowly turning in his huddled posture, Reginald observed one of his guards, a seasoned soldier named John, challenging Edwin with an upraised shortsword.

A dagger had materialized in Edwin's hand, and this minor accessory transformed his appearance from that of a servant to that of an assassin. The sun reflected from the sharp blade as the men took measure of each other.

Roger was already firmly in hand. He had apparently not been prepared for the timing of the attack or the speed of the reaction. Reginald's guards had become sadly accustomed to being alert to potential assassins.

"Didn't have a good feeling about this one," one of Reginald's guards explained with a tug at Roger's arms that made him groan.

"Then I am thankful that you heeded the urging of the Holy Spirit," Reginald replied, remembering how he shoved aside his own concerns, certain that he was being overly cautious.

Their comments were cut short by Edwin's sudden movement, a lunge toward John that almost made Reginald's heart stop. Stepping back from the fray, Reginald almost fell over due to his awkwardly hunched position. Moving to put his horse's body between himself and the fight, he pulled himself up and peered over the horse's back.

The men were deftly parrying each other's fierce slashes. However, Reginald realized just a moment before the would-be assassin that it was only a distraction. While they had numbered only two, Reginald's guard was a score. There was no need to allow the battle to end fairly.

Two more guards had circled around Edwin as he fought for his life. It seemed too easy then for them to simply coordinate grasping his arms and holding fast.

"We will truss them up good," John assured Reginald with a firm nod. He casually slid his blade into a hidden sheath and added his opponent's to a saddlebag, continuing, "You can deal with them when we arrive in Viterbo."

Reginald, still in shock, mumbled more thanks for the shortsword skills that had saved him, but John shrugged off the praise as if fighting for his life were part of the daily routine.

Alvise took charge of sorting out the men and their horses

as Reginald remounted. His mind was spinning with what could have happened due to his lack of foresight. "The Lord is with me if I would only be a better listener," he mumbled to himself.

Once they were again on the move, Alvise sidled up to him. "Reg, are you alright?"

Offering him a small, unconvincing smile, Reginald promised that he was unharmed.

"I know that, for I was there. No need to be stoic with me, my friend."

Reginald's smile grew genuine, and he said, "I am simply disappointed, Alvise. In myself for failing to anticipate the plot and with my cousin for continuing in his sinful striving for revenge."

"I do not believe the King of England believes he is capable of sinning. What type of man must one be to form a church solely to put yourself at the head of it?"

Reginald just shook his head. He had spent years sparring with Henry and praying for answers. None had come to him.

"Do not worry," Alvise encouraged him in a softer voice. "God protects you. He has kept you from King Henry's assassins time and again. He will not abandon you now."

"Thank you, Alvise. We all need a good friend to remind us of these truths at times."

They rode on in companionable silence. Thankfully, the balance of the trip was uneventful. By the time they arrived at the home allocated to Reginald in Viterbo, he was able to appreciate the beauty of the rolling hills and comfortable quarters. He would leave the question of what to do with his inept assassins till the morrow.

~ ~ ~ ~

Reginald rose well before dawn in order to enjoy the sunrise from his new home. It was an ideal time to spend in prayer while much of the household was still abed. He could hear the distant muffled sounds of kitchen servants, who must rise early to provide the rest of them with food to break their fast, but he was mostly enveloped in silence.

Within that silence, he found an answer to the dilemma of his prisoners. Later he shared it with Alvise.

"I would like them sent back to England."

Alvise had been about to place a piece of fluffy manchet loaf into his mouth, but his hand paused inches from his open lips. He slowly lowered the bread to his plate and peered at Reginald.

"They should be hanged."

Reginald was already nodding in anticipation of his words. "I understand that, but I wish to show myself to be a better man than my cousin, the king. I would have mercy on these men to give greater glory to God."

"Hmmmm...." Alvise sat back and considered the plan with his mouth clamped tightly shut. He did not often speak against Reginald, and as governor of Viterbo it was his decision what happened to criminals within the jurisdiction.

"I would also build a chapel at the roadside where God saved me from the hands of the assassins," Reginald added to break into his friend's thoughts. "It is an ideal location for pilgrims to rest and pray upon the road to Rome. They will be able to refresh themselves before they enter the city."

Reginald knew he had won Alvise over when he leaned forward and took up his food again. "Very well, Reg. Henry is unlikely to change his course regardless of what you do with these two. However, they will be eternally grateful and will praise the name of Reginald Pole wherever they go."

"I would rather they praise the name of God," Reginald countered.

Alvise laughed and cut more bread from the fresh baked loaf. "Then you had better preach to them before they leave as well, my friend."

Reginald looked out the window while his friend's laughter abated. A young girl was feeding chickens in the yard. She leaned over to pet them as if they were dogs, and Reginald hoped she would not have to assist in their butchering.

February 1542

Life in Viterbo fell into a calm routine that suited Reginald. Friends from Rome visited often enough to please him and keep Alvise from becoming bored. Michelangelo Buonarroti, the artist, had come to escort their mutual friend Vittoria Colonna to Viterbo, and Reginald had been pleased with the opportunity of edifying conversation they had shared.

Before his friendship with Buonarroti, Reginald had never considered the faith involved in creating artwork, even that prepared for the Vatican. Listening to Michelangelo speak – almost preaching – about the messages within his work, Reginald was humbled by how much he had to learn. When next in Rome, he would examine the paintings within the Sistine Chapel with greater care.

Realizing that his mind had wandered from the book in his hand all the way to Rome, Reginald set aside the volume. He stood and stretched his stiff spine before heading toward the hall to see that preparations were well underway for another visit.

Gasparo Contarini would be staying in Viterbo for a few days on his way to Spain, and Reginald looked forward to sharing with him some of the topics he had discussed with Michelangelo. Vittoria was no less an inspiring conversationalist with an active and independent mind. She had stayed on at the convent in Viterbo when Michelangelo was forced to return to projects in Rome.

The first thing she had said to Reginald upon arrival was, "I shall serve as your mother now." She said it matter-of-factly, but Reginald knew that shared grief and sympathy gave her words a higher value than most of the empty words of condolences he had received in the past months.

In truth, Vittoria had already been much like a mother to him even while his own had yet lived, for Margaret Pole had been in England while Vittoria was here in Italy. She loved to learn from Reginald, but also was unafraid to challenge his ideas. When he convinced her of a point, she beamed at him with pride rather than anger that she had been proven wrong.

Reginald noticed Vittoria's small, wiry frame approaching as though his thoughts had conjured her bodily.

"Mother Colonna," he murmured kneeling before her to receive her blessing. Vittoria was only just old enough to be Reginald's mother at fifteen years his senior, but the roles suited them.

"God be with you, Reginald," she rasped, then waited for him to stand and bless her in return. "Have you heard from your brother?" she asked when the short ritual was complete.

"Geoffrey?" Reginald asked unnecessarily, realizing as he said it that Geoffrey was his only brother who still walked upon the earth. "He remains in England, as far as I know. With the king's pardon, he may eventually receive some of my family's titles."

"He should not gamble the safety of his wife and children upon that pardon," Vittoria said, wagging a finger at Reginald as if it were his decision.

"I have not communicated with him," Reginald pointed out, feeling the need to defend himself. "I must admit that I am somewhat surprised that he has not found his way to safety here."

"Perhaps he does not know if he would be welcome."

Reginald began to protest before realizing that she was correct. Geoffrey had given evidence to the King that had sent their brother, Henry, and later their mother to the scaffold. "I must let him know that he is forgiven and welcome," Reginald stated. Now that the truth was before him, he wished to immediately be at the task.

"That is good," Vittoria agreed with a small smile and single nod. She knew that Reginald might take days or even weeks to formulate the words that he wished to share with his younger brother and even longer to employ a messenger who could hope to deliver the missive without King Henry's knowledge, but he would see it done.

When Cardinal Gasparo Contarini arrived a few days later, he came bearing more horrifying news from England.

"He has executed another queen," Contarini divulged as they relaxed over wine and sweetmeats his first evening in Viterbo. A flush rose to cover his cheeks and his hand shook slightly at the thought.

"Catherine Howard?" Reginald cried. He fleetingly wondered how many of the world's kings had so many wives that it was difficult to keep track of them, even as he imagined the sweet, young woman led up a scaffold. He placed his wine glass on the table. Its taste had become bitter.

"That is the word in Rome," Contarini affirmed with a sad nod. "He breaks each of God's laws in turn as he claims to be his representative," he added passionately.

Reginald took in his friend's face, tightened by anger, but also something more. Gasparo had aged in the few months since they had last seen each other in Rome. The time was not right to inquire after his health, so he turned his thoughts back to the most recent unfortunate Tudor queen.

"What charges were brought against her?"

Contarini scoffed. "Does it matter?" He shook his head with his chin almost upon his chest. "Forgive me, Reginald," he said. "I believe I was wrong when I advised you that your response to King Henry was too harsh. You were almost prophetic in your words to him, and since then he has only drawn further from God."

Saying nothing, Reginald simply laid his hand upon his friend's for a moment, long enough to let him know he understood and held no grudges.

"She was charged with adultery, just as the Boleyn witch was."

His lips pressed into a thin line as Reginald considered this. Had Catherine committed adultery? He was almost certain that Anne never had, though she had long before proven herself a whore in breaking up Henry's true marriage. Catherine Howard was young, impetuous, and beautiful. She had been married to an aged, tempestuous tyrant. Only God knew the truth.

"Where will it all end?" Reginald whispered. "How many good people will be sacrificed on the altar of the false god, Henry Tudor?"

Contarini's eyes widened. He was always afraid of saying something ungodly, and that fear extended to his more outspoken friend. "Reginald, take care," he murmured, though the admonishment carried little force. He wondered the same thing, even if he would not have uttered the words.

Suddenly, Reginald leaned forward, his eyes flashing. "Gasparo, you have participated in more efforts toward reconciliation than anyone. You were at Worms, Ratisbon, and Regensberg. Do you see good Christian people coming together against the antichrist in England?"

The older man's eyebrows arched, and he took a deep breath. Before he could respond, Reginald asked another question.

"Did you meet Martin Luther?"

It seemed that Contarini would be shaking his head all evening. "At Worms, I only heard of his infamous stance after the fact. How I wish now that I had spoken to him back in 1521! Maybe we would be closer to reconciliation now. I have heard that Luther only grows more irascible and less open to compromise with age."

Reginald sighed. "I have heard the same. The pains and curses that come with old age can destroy the personality of those who suffer them."

"Too true," Contarini agreed. "Maybe that is also a problem for your English king."

With a frown and raised eyebrow, Reginald sat back and considered this. "Having not seen the king with my own eyes these many years, I believe I am in the habit of envisioning him as a young man. However, you are correct. He would be of an age with Luther. A bit younger," he added as he saw Gasparo prepare to correct him, "but he has also led a more physically demanding life."

"Still," Contarini said in dismay, "there is no excuse for chopping off the head of not one but two wives."

"There you have the right of it," Reginald agreed before they both settled back into silence with their thoughts.

The few days of Contarini's visit seemed to fly, and Reginald had a curious feeling of time slipping through his fingers that he could not shake. It caused him to examine the men he passed on the street and sweep the candlelight around his chamber at night as if scaring off a ghost. He did not wish to ignore nudges from his guardian angel, but nothing seemed amiss.

He did not share his premonition with anyone, for he had little more than a nervousness in his gut to offer as evidence. Therefore, as he joined the small crowd that gathered to see Contarini and his party off, he smiled and shook hands as enthusiastically as Alvise.

"Do write us from Spain," Alvise was congenially demanding, and Gasparo's head bobbed in agreement.

"And let me know what word you receive from your brother," Contarini said, turning to Reginald. "It is good for brothers to be reconciled."

Reginald bit down on his lip, knowing that Gasparo meant much more than the relationship between he and Geoffrey, but he had no vision of how to bring Catholic and Protestant brothers and sisters back together. Even the joint statement on unification of the previous summer had not helped them make the strides he had hoped it would.

"Take care of yourself, Gasparo," Reginald said, taking the older man's hands in his own. "Enjoy the sunny warmth of Spain."

"That I shall, dear friend. Until we meet again."

Reginald only nodded in response. Something in Gasparo's eyes caused a lump to rise in his throat. With a somber nod, Gasparo flicked the reins held loosely in his hands and began the slow journey toward Spain.

August 1542

The sun was high and bright in the sky, but it could not eradicate the chill that emanated from Reginald's heart. He should not be strolling down the dusty path on his own. Strangers who were suspected of being assassins, or at the very least spies, of King Henry VIII had been spotted creeping around Viterbo in recent weeks. Had pardoning the last pair made these bolder? At the moment, he did not care.

He had heard that Thomas Wyatt had vowed to his king that he would see Reginald dead or imprisoned, but even the surprising wrath and ambition of the poet could not cause fear or caution to rise in Reginald this day. Heaven felt too real and close.

Word had arrived that Gasparo Contarini had died in Spain, and Reginald could not bring himself to feel concern for his own mortality as he grieved for his friend. Contarini had been with him in Venice when Reginald received the news that Geoffrey was imprisoned within the Tower of London. That had been the moment that Reginald had fully understood the tyranny of the English king and the danger his family was in.

Gasparo had prayed with Reginald and comforted him as Henry moved against increasing numbers of Reginald's extended family, finally executing his eldest brother, Lord Montague, and cousin, Henry Courtenay. His mother had also been imprisoned at that point, but it had been too late to make amends. The king was set on vengeance.

Reginald looked up and realized that his feet had automatically carried him to the cathedral. He could feel closer to his friend and his God within the strong, unchanging walls.

He entered the cavernous structure and felt immediately comforted by the cloud of witnesses he was certain surrounded him. Making his way to a simple wooden bench, Reginald sat with the intention of prayer. However, memories of Gasparo flooded his mind, making conversation with God impossible. Or maybe those memories were God's message to him in that moment.

Remembering Gasparo's desire for reconciliation with the Protestants that he had not lived to see made Reginald frown. His friend had worked fervently toward that admirable goal. Why would God take him from it? Then his mind was filled with a vision of Gasparo blushing furiously at the most innocent of innuendoes. He would shake at the thought of sin and be shocked that others took pleasure in it. A smile finally curved upon Reginald's lips at the memory.

He remained seated, eyes closed in order to feel part of the next world rather than the one that surrounded him, as the sun set and a chill crept into the sanctuary. Only when that cold tightened its icy grip on Reginald's joints did he finally realize that full dark had settled upon Viterbo. The walk home would be even more perilous than his earlier trek.

Reginald stood, his knees creaking in complaint. It surprised him that he had been left to his own thoughts for such an extended period. A few candles had been lit within the church, but he had not heard a footstep or whisper. Alvise must have spread the word of his mourning and instructed the townspeople to leave their supplications for another day.

The air did not hold quite the same chill when he stepped outside, and for this he was thankful. Remnants of summer warmth seemed to rise from the stone path and hide the eaves of the cottages he passed. Reginald kept a sharp eye on dark corners and sunken doorways, but fear did not creep into his heart, so he felt certain that he was safe for tonight.

Upon arriving home, he found that he was saved for his Father's work. The Pope had summoned him to represent his interests in Trent that October.

May 1543

Reginald was not certain what he had hoped to achieve in Trent after so many others had failed at reconciliation since Martin Luther had written his Ninety-five Theses a quarter-century earlier. Or did their current confrontation find its roots all the way back in the Great Schism of the fourteenth century? Reginald was unsure when it had started or if it would ever end. Exhaustion overwhelmed him as Viterbo finally came into sight.

The council, if it could even be called that, had been plagued by delays, poor attendance, and worse attitudes. Reginald arrived home seven months after leaving it, having achieved nothing. The serene landscape promised rest but brought him no joy.

He had failed. Just as he had failed with the King of England, he had failed to bring the German Protestants to reconciliation. He knew not why God kept providing him with work that he was clearly not equipped to perform.

As the tired and saddle-sore party halted in the courtyard of Reginald's home, he missed the encouraging, optimistic presence of Alvise. While Reginald had been called to Trent, his friend had been summoned to Rome. Finding his spirits so low, Reginald had a new appreciation for the sunny disposition that Alvise was unfailingly able to maintain.

The next morning, Reginald rose refreshed if not rejuvenated. Sharing a simple morning meal with Vittoria, he was finally given reason to shake off his dark mood.

"Our friend, Michelangelo, has written that he will arrive from Rome within the fortnight," she shared as she gingerly pulled apart sections of an orange.

"That is good news!" Reginald exclaimed with a smile as juice squirted onto Vittoria's tunic despite her best efforts. "I am eager to hear how his work progresses in the Pauline Chapel."

"As am I, Reginald," she muttered, rubbing pointlessly at the stickiness. "You, though, will one day be blessed to see it, while I will never be allowed in such a hallowed place."

A thoughtful frown creased Reginald's face. He had never considered the greater gain that would come from artwork displayed for all to see rather than only the select few of the highest ranks within the Vatican.

"I shall take you inside the Sistine Chapel," he offered her as consolation and was rewarded by a grin that forced laughlines into greater prominence.

"When we are next in Rome," she ordered.

He dipped his head to her. "You have my word, Mother Colonna" he promised.

With Alvise in Rome, Viterbo was quiet, and Reginald found it easier than he had anticipated to catch up on work that had been set aside during his time in Trent. Simple meals, often with Vittoria as his only guest, and hours in his study helped ease his disappointment over the failed council. Therefore, he was in higher spirits when his friend arrived.

Offering a shallow bow from the portico, Reginald greeted Michelangelo as servants helped him dismount.

"Welcome, my friend! Vittoria will be overjoyed that you are here at last."

"She was worried?" Michelangelo asked as he ran fingers through disheveled grey hair and smoothed his wrinkled tunic. "I have told her that an artist is always on time. However, all things occur only on his own time."

Michelangelo had made his way to Reginald as he spoke, and they clasped hands heartily, each grinning at the image of their Vittoria the exchange brought to mind. She acted in much the same capacity of adopted mother to each of them, though Michelangelo was the oldest of the trio by far. Before anything more could be said, she appeared as if sensing her dear one's presence.

"Thank the Lord and his saints that you have arrived safely," she exclaimed with hands raised toward heaven. Michelangelo released Reginald's hand in order to envelop Vittoria in an embrace before bowing his head for her blessing. "Ah, you are a good boy," she murmured as he rose, as if referring to a small child rather than a man of almost seventy years of age. The fact that he was older than Vittoria was no obstacle at all to her mothering.

The two had long been friends, sharing drawings, paintings, and lines of verse since they were young enough for people to wonder if they had a romantic attachment. At one time, Reginald was certain, that had been Michelangelo's hope, but each had settled into their old age content with the friendship God had granted them. The elderly artist offered Vittoria his arm, and she fondly grasped it, while Reginald followed them inside.

Seated around the table as the sun began its decline in the sky, Reginald and Vittoria listened intently as Michelangelo spoke of his work on the Pauline Chapel murals.

"I used to strive for aesthetic perfection," his low voice rumbled as he examined the wine in his glass, "but I have come to realize that the message is where art's true value lies." He sat forward as he warmed to his topic. "When someone looks at these paintings long after I am dead, I want them to see my faith in our Lord in heaven!" he exclaimed gesturing upward with the glass. "The message of faith is vital and timeless. Hundreds of years from now, someone might take in my works and nod, saying 'Whoever painted this – that man believed in God.'"

"'That man' you say," Reginald noted. "You do not believe you will be remembered for your art?"

Michelangelo waved the question off with such vigor that he almost spilled his wine. "It does not matter! We are all dust and shall return to our Father. What is important is that we share that truth. I must do it with my art, just as you must with your writing."

"But I am a cardinal of the church," Reginald countered. "Surely, God has made it my calling to be about his work."

"Ah," Michelangelo nodded with a grin. "Is it not the work that he calls each one of us to?" He sat back, took a sip, and continued. "As the monk Luther has said, 'none of us is born an apostle, preacher, teacher, pastor; but there all of us are born solely priests.'"

Reginald shook his head in good-natured dismay. "You would quote Martin Luther to me?" he asked. "That man has caused more trouble in our lifetime than even England's king."

"But has he?" Vittoria piped up. "He has encouraged us to think and to pray. Is this such a horrible thing?" she asked as Michelangelo nodded his head in agreement.

"I know you must tell me the man is a heretic," Michelangelo said with a lopsided grin that filled his face with deep wrinkles, "but, Reginald, you must admit. The man makes some good points."

With a laugh, he shook his head, "I shall do no such thing." He lifted the glass to his lips to halt anything else he might say.

"But you must!" Vittoria insisted, almost jumping out of her seat in her passion. "What would you say to his philosophy that we are saved by faith alone?"

She pinned him with her eyes, and Reginald understood that he could not joke his way out of this quandary. What did he think? More importantly, what could he say that would not come back to haunt him?

"Vittoria, this is what I think," he began with a deep breath. "I believe God would have us believe as firmly as if our salvation depended upon faith alone and act as if good works were all sufficient."

"Hear! Hear!" Michelangelo cheered, and Reginald was grateful that the conversation relaxed into less controversial topics.

June 1543

Not long after Michelangelo's departure, Reginald's brother, Geoffrey unexpectedly appeared. Reginald had received no response to the letter he had so painstakingly written and sent at great expense, but it had clearly been delivered. Geoffrey arrived in Viterbo with little besides the clothes on his back and threw himself into his older brother's arms.

Reginald had tried to ask about Constance, Geoffrey's wife, and their children, but his brother was offering little information. He seemed content to sit at Reginald's table and spend his days in leisurely pursuits. Geoffrey whined with the skill of a spoiled child to pressure Reginald into spending more time away from his studies and prayers than he preferred.

After a few weeks of this routine, Reginald rose early in order to make his way to the cathedral undetected. He needed the time to center himself and pray for his brother. The hours spent in the cool semi-darkness were a balm to his soul, but it was not long before sounds announcing he was not alone came from the narthex.

Only Geoffrey, would so carelessly intrude upon another man's devotions. Yet, he was the only brother Reginald had remaining in this world, he reminded himself with a sigh.

The brothers shared few features. Geoffrey looked like their father who had died shortly before he was born. His hair was always tousled as if he had just risen from bed and fell in dark waves around his friendly face. His deep brown eyes frequently reminded Reginald of a wounded dog. Reginald took after their mother with his dark auburn hair and eyes that could not decide if they were green or blue. He also shared her tall, thin stature and imperious habit of holding his head up in a manner that suggested a crown could balance upon it.

In spite of himself and in spite of everything Geoffrey had

done, Reginald could not help but smile at him now. He had missed the comfort of family during his long years in France and Italy. Whatever his faults, Geoffrey was loved by his older brother.

"What is it, Geoffrey, that causes you to interrupt my prayers?" Reginald asked calmly enough that the words carried no true accusation.

"Your prayers are just what I wish to discuss," Geoffrey said with an eager smile.

"Truly?" Reginald inquired with an upraised eyebrow. He had no idea how much this reminded Geoffrey of their mother.

"Well, sort of," Geoffrey admitted, looking down at his scuffed shoes. A new light was in his eyes when he finally looked up and met his brother's gaze. "I wish to seek absolution from the Pope. You could take me before him!"

Reginald held up a hand before Geoffrey could continue with the details of his plan. He almost shook his head, shocked at how much his middle-aged brother sounded like a small boy explaining the rules of a game he had just invented.

Before Geoffrey's face could fall in rejection, Reginald spoke, "It must be God's will for you to do so, for I have just been summoned to Rome. You may accompany me."

Geoffrey moved forward and grasped both of Reginald's hands in his own. "Thank you, brother," he whispered huskily. "You have no idea what this means to me."

Taken aback by his brother's seriousness, Reginald found that he could not form the words he wished to say before Geoffrey had casually turned and strolled out of the sanctuary.

They were upon the road to Rome when Reginald decided to speak to Geoffrey of his family. "Do you hear from Constance?" he asked.

Joy seemed to drain from Geoffrey's face at the mention of his wife, who remained in England. "How could I? The king allows us no communication."

Reginald nodded. His letters from his brothers and mother had been read by members of the king's council, long ago when he had a mother and elder brother to write to him.

"You must have some news of her," he pressed. "After all, you were fully pardoned. Surely, she is permitted to write."

"She does not," Geoffrey stated flatly.

Reginald decided to press him no further at this time but did begin to wonder if his brother planned on returning to England and his wife.

They had shared little other conversation as they traveled. Reginald utilized the time to instruct Geoffrey on his behavior before the Holy Father, but the remainder of the trip had been spent in silence. It seemed that, though they were brothers, Reginald and Geoffrey had little in common, and they enjoyed few shared memories that could be pulled out and reexamined for the sake of discussion.

Therefore, they were both relieved to see the horizon become jagged with the buildings of Rome. Geoffrey exhibited some nervousness regarding his audience with the Pope, which Reginald did nothing to alleviate. It was right for him to feel some anxiety over his sin until it was pardoned.

Without any more delay than was necessary for settling into their quarters and making themselves presentable, the brothers strode purposefully through the corridor that led to the private chapel of Pope Paul III.

Plans to travel to Rome had been made in haste, so few knew to expect Reginald. He would send word to his friends, but only after he had seen to the absolution of his brother. Geoffrey had given the evidence that had led to the deaths of their brother and mother, as well as Henry Courtenay and Edward Neville. The repercussions upon wives and families was immeasurable. It was good for him to seek forgiveness.

Maybe, once it was given, Reginald could fully forgive him as well.

Geoffrey appeared contrite as he walked slowly toward the white robed figure. Reginald stood off to one side, a silent observer of the sacred rite. Reaching the steps that would take him to the dais, Geoffrey lowered himself to the ground. Stretching his arms wide, he remained facedown as Pope Paul whispered prayers above and around him that did not reach Reginald's ears but certainly reached God's.

Eventually, he must have been instructed to rise, because Geoffrey did so and moved to a prie-dieu to kneel. Reginald could see the Holy Father place a hand upon his brother's head and hear their voices exchange responses without making out the words of his brother's confession.

Only when Paul pronounced, "I offer you absolution in the name of the Father, Son, and Holy Spirit. Your sins are forgiven. Rise and sin no more," were any words of the ceremony loud enough for Reginald to hear.

Geoffrey stood, and his eyes immediately found his brother. Reginald remained somber as he slowly moved toward him, but Geoffrey was beaming. Until he saw his brother's frown. Then Geoffrey arranged his face into a more suitably penitent expression.

He held his peace long enough for them to silently leave the chapel before exclaiming, "I feel as though a great burden has been lifted from my shoulders!"

Reginald furrowed his brow at Geoffrey's exuberance, but said, "That is good. God does not want our guilt to keep us from good works. His forgiveness is a great mercy."

"Yes, it is!" Geoffrey cried, swinging his arms as he walked. He looked as though he would skip and dance if his older brother were not at his side.

Reginald wondered why this bothered him. It was good and right that the soul feel freedom from the weight of sin upon repentance. He realized that he doubted Geoffrey's sincerity, and this made him angry at himself. Only God could judge the authenticity of Geoffrey's confession, and he must be content with that. In the midst of his internal meanderings, he realized that his brother had continued speaking.

"....must be some post you could recommend me for," Geoffrey finished, but Reginald had no need to ask him to repeat the rest.

"You desire a position in Rome?" Reginald asked, watching his brother soaking in the bustle of the city with excitement in his eyes.

"Of course," Geoffrey replied. "I understand why you prefer Viterbo," he added as though he was afraid he had offered offence. "However, I believe I am more suited to Rome."

"I see," Reginald muttered noncommittally. "And what of Constance?"

Geoffrey shrugged. "She is a strong woman. Good at taking care of herself."

"And your children?"

"Practically grown," Geoffrey countered. Suddenly, he halted his steps and spun to face his brother. "You do not want me here."

"It is not my decision," Reginald evaded with his palms raised. "I can inquire regarding suitable positions for you if you do not plan a return to England."

Geoffrey's energy left him, and he whispered, "You understand, Reginald. I cannot go back. The King...."

He let his voice trail off, and Reginald did understand. Geoffrey was terrified. He may be forgiven of the sins he had committed under torture at the order of Henry VIII, but Geoffrey knew his weaknesses, knew that he would be questioned after spending time with his brother, and knew that he was not up to the task.

"I will find something for you," Reginald promised. But not in Rome, he added silently to himself.

He realized the extent of the stress his brother's presence placed upon him when he finally had the opportunity to relax for an evening with Cardinal Bembo. It was a beautiful summer evening, so they were seated on a rooftop veranda with a decanter of wine between them.

Reginald released a sigh as tension left his shoulders and the sun cast a riot of color into the sky.

"You have not been reading your Cicero," Pietro observed.

Reginald had closed his eyes to soak up the peaceful feeling, but he opened them to peer at his friend. "How can you tell?"

"Ha! It is easy to see that you are far too filled with anxiety to have been studying the ancients. You are stuck firmly in the present with all its worries," Bembo waved his hands as though this was all as clear to see as if Michelangelo had painted it on the wall.

With a grin, Reginald admitted, "As usual, you are correct, Pietro." He took a deep draught from his glass and refilled it before speaking again. "It is my brother."

Bembo nodded solemnly. "It can be a heavy burden to be our brothers' keeper as is commanded by our Lord. Geoffrey has many demons."

"He does," Reginald agreed. "I must have greater patience with him."

"Ah, Reynaldo," Bembo said affectionately, leaning over to pat Reginald's knee. "You would take on the world believing it was your duty." Shaking his head, he continued, "The Bishop of Liege is in need of a man to see to duties of which I believe your brother would be capable."

"Send him to Flanders?" Reginald asked, sitting upright, his muscles tightening with the discussion of his brother.

Before he could disagree, Bembo cut him off. "Yes, Flanders would be ideal. You may send him an allowance if it eases your conscience, but you are not obligated to keep him at your own table."

"What if he...." Reginald realized he did not know what he was afraid of Geoffrey doing. Saying the wrong thing? Ending up in prison?

"Reynaldo, your brother is his own man, not your child. You will arrange this agreeable position for him and consider your obligation fulfilled."

He nodded and lifted his glass to his lips, the matter closed.

November 1543

When Reginald next traveled to Rome some months later, it was without Geoffrey at his side. His adventurous younger brother was disappointed to be sent away but had few options to consider. Reginald was hopeful that Geoffrey would see the sense of the decision once he was settled in Flanders. Geoffrey's future, and that of his family, Reginald had forced himself to give up to God.

He took comfort in a stop at the chapel he had built to thank God for his deliverance from assassins four years earlier. The chapel was not magnificent, certainly not when compared to the wonders of Rome, but it was well placed and cozy.

It was a small, round structure with pillars placed only a few feet apart, evenly dividing the circumference into eight equal sections. The domed roof was covered with terracotta tiles in varied shades of red and yellow that made it appear that the sun was always setting atop of the building. One entered through their choice of two doors. A structure of this size required only one, but Reginald's experience with assassins had left him with a justifiable fear of becoming trapped.

The interior was simple, with a few benches and plain altar. It was all pilgrims would need as they rested for their final stop before entering Rome. Reginald prayed and refreshed himself just as he hoped others did when their path led them to this chapel. He thought of Michelangelo leaving his artwork for future generations and was uplifted by the fact that he, at least, left this small monument.

On this peaceful day, it was difficult to believe that Reginald had almost met his demise on this very spot. Had God demanded his life, he would, of course, had been happy to offer it up. But that offer did not extend to King Henry of England. Upon this reflection, Reginald gave thanks that he had not had any recent visitors sent by his vengeful cousin. Since Henry had arrested

Thomas Wyatt, his own spy and one of many sent against Reginald, there had been no further threats.

That prayer sent heavenward, Reginald left the chapel to join his party and cover the last few miles of their journey. He admitted only to himself that he was more eager to see Michelangelo's progress within the Pauline Chapel than he was to hear what mission that titular Paul had for him next.

~ ~ ~ ~

"You wish for me to return to Trent?"

It took all of Reginald's self-control to avoid shaking his head in dismay. It had been less than a year since his departure from Trent. The only results had been disappointment, and he had no desire for a repeat performance.

"The council will succeed," Paul insisted. "We must remain steadfast in this."

Reginald understood why the Pope desired to have a representative in Trent, but he did not wish to be the one sent.

"How rarely those God has chosen to send have felt equipped for their task," Paul pointed out, sensing Reginald's reluctance.

Suppressing a sigh, Reginald nodded his agreement with his lips pressed into a thin line. He felt his time was being wasted more than his lack of talent, but he could not deny that he was afraid of failure as well. Therefore, he would go as God directed him rather than where he wished.

"I do appreciate your efforts and trustworthiness," the Pope added in an attempt to soothe him.

"That is very gracious of you, but it is my duty," Reginald replied. He humbly bowed his head. It was not for him to doubt the judgement of Christ's representative on earth.

Leaving the presence of the Pope, Reginald found his way to the new chapel where Michelangelo was at work. His brisk steps and promise of time with a dear friend helped release the tension that had stiffened the muscles of his back.

Words of greeting caught in Reginald's throat as he entered the chapel. He came to an abrupt halt and stared wide-eyed at the fresco before him. Michelangelo was precariously balanced upon scaffolding that no man in their seventies should dare to climb, but Reginald could not even form a word of warning. He was captivated by the image of Saul upon the road to Damascus.

The power of God, held within a bright beam of light, poured down from heaven to the frightened soul fallen in the road. The cowering figure was surrounded by others who seemed uncertain of the miracle taking place in their presence. The room was somewhat dark, but the artist had planned the scene so that sunlight shone upon the golden paint with breathtaking impact.

Reginald marveled at the image. If a recreation of this moment conjured this much wonder, what it must have been like to be present as Saul became Paul!

"Why, Reginald," Michelangelo cried, "you should have spoken! You will cause an old man to be frightened to death!"

Realizing that his jaw had dropped, Reginald clamped his mouth shut and forced his eyes to move from the painting to his friend. He smiled as Michelangelo spritely climbed from his perch.

"If you are not afraid to scale that scaffolding, you should have no fear of me," Reginald asserted as the artist reached the floor.

Michelangelo gazed up as if considering this before shrugging. "I shall meet my end as our Lord sees fit, whatever the cause," he said, stepping to Reginald's side and taking in his work from the same point of view. They both simply stood there, reliving the moment of Saul's conversion.

Reginald discovered that he was hoping for that beam of light to find him upon his own road to Trent, that the power of

God might guide him in this seemingly hopeless clash with the reformers. Then he shook his head. What arrogance to think of himself worthy of the same miracle as Saint Paul!

"No one was less worthy than Saul," Michelangelo murmured softly as if reading Reginald's thoughts. "Can you imagine? This persecutor of Christians receiving blessing and forgiveness directly from God?"

Tilting his head, Reginald considered this. In the cacophony of color, his eyes found intricate details in the figures. Fear on one face, awe upon another. Heavenly beings watched in anticipation.

Directly from God, his friend had said. He tilted his head the other way and let those words meander through his mind. Saul had no need of a pope, cardinal, or even country priest. Reginald was not sure where this idea was taking him, but Michelangelo was speaking, so he set it aside.

They spent almost an hour discussing the work and the artist's reasons for including certain aspects. However, Reginald could not convince him to divulge what image would fill the opposing wall.

"That is one that your friend, the Pope, may not like," Michelangelo admitted, mischievous grin in place.

"Then I look forward to seeing it," Reginald said.

He could not disguise his shock mingled with respect that someone would purposefully challenge Pope Paul, but if any man could without consequence, it was Michelangelo. Authority had already been determined between them when Michelangelo refused to add more gold leaf to the Sistine Chapel. Yet, here the artist was with another large commission. Michelangelo knew his worth.

"I look forward to it, indeed," Reginald repeated, and the two men dragged their eyes from Saint Paul to give each other a sidelong glance and grin.

September 1544

The sky was brightening from pale pink to a warm yellow as Reginald sat at his desk considering the document before him. If he believed that his assignment to Trent was hopeless before, how much more so now that he read the words that would be read by countless others. The latest tract from Martin Luther did not encourage reconciliation in the least.

Reginald released a deep sigh as he flipped back to the cover. It made no secret of the small book's contents. *Against the Papacy formed by the Devil.* Reginald shook his head and rubbed his face wearily.

His eyes burned from examining the pages so closely before he had good light, and his heart was filled with dismay at the lack of concern for unity found within. Even if Reginald was willing to accept the truth of some of Luther's original theses, anger stirred within him at the confrontational nature of the reformer's strategy. Could he not see that division within the church would serve none?

"Is there truly no hope for us?" he asked as his eyes searched the beams of his study's ceiling.

Nothing is impossible with God. The thought echoed in his mind, but it was washed away by a heavy wave of doubt.

Longer study of the document would gain him nothing, so Reginald stood. His back was stiff and his stomach empty, so he decided to walk to the kitchen to stretch his muscles and find a morsel for breaking his fast.

As Reginald was strolling outside, breaking pieces of bread from the small loaf he had been given, a messenger approached. He immediately recognized the seal as that belonging to Alvise. He grinned, thinking this missive would contain some good news to lift his spirits.

He covered the ground in returning to his study at a quicker pace than he had left and broke the seal as soon as he was seated.

However, his grin faded as he read.

Reginald knew that the King of England had landed his troops at Calais two months earlier, but the fall of Boulogne was news to him. The line that truly filled his heart with dread was one that Alvise had likely penned without considering the full impact it would have on his good friend.

"The rumor is, dear Reg, that old Hal expects you to confront him at the head of Papal troops."

And so, Reginald acknowledged, he was not yet rid of the animosity of Henry VIII and all that he had the power to bring down upon him.

April 1545

Reginald's reaction to Luther's tract had been titled *De Concilio*. More than anything else, he wished to see reconciliation between the Church and the Reformers. It was for this reason that he prepared to travel to Trent, despite his reservations regarding the proposed council.

Making matters worse, he was forced to travel separate from his comrades. Cardinals Del Monte, Carafa, and Cervini had left Rome days earlier and taken a different route than that planned by Reginald's entourage, for assassination threats had been renewed with King Henry's activity on the Continent.

As Reginald prepared to leave Viterbo with his horseman guard made up of twenty-five of the Pope's best men, he struggled to remain optimistic about the trip's purpose. A man of God should not have to travel secret routes surrounded by bodyguards. What message did that send to those who witnessed them along the way? Yet, he knew not what else he could do.

Vittoria and Alvise stood side by side, ready to say their farewells. Lines of worry were engraved across Vittoria's countenance, but Alvise seemed as cheerful as always. His grin forced an answering one from Reginald.

"How I wish you traveled with me," Reginald said, holding Alvise's hand between his own. "Your hopefulness is a balm to my pessimism."

"Then I will write often to encourage you. I would not want you to return to Viterbo as an ornery curmudgeon."

Reginald laughed and turned to Vittoria, whose face had not softened with the jest. He embraced her gently and asked that she care for his household in his absence. He knew it was unnecessary, but he did not wish to address the reasons for the concern etched upon her features.

"Be careful, Reginald," she ordered.

Reginald gestured to the men waiting for him. "I am."

Vittoria gave the troop a dismissive glance and took up Reginald's hand. "God is with you. Do not ignore his nudges," she insisted. "Stay safe and return to us."

Reginald smiled gently. "I believe I have a greater assignment than simply surviving," he said.

Vittoria shook her head. "You may be a voice of reason among the angry voices, but they will be raised too high to hear you."

His brows raised in surprise, Reginald took a moment to respond. "You do not believe reconciliation is possible, Vittoria? But you are devout in your own faith that includes some wisdom of the reformers."

She nodded yet maintained, "But these men do not come together to reconcile. They go to argue. The quiet voice of reason will be ignored."

"That is enough of that!" Alvise broke in, forcing himself between Reginald and Vittoria. "We shall set Reg upon his journey with encouraging words and godspeed."

"Of course," Vittoria agreed, bowing her head at the rebuke, as gently as it came from Alvise.

"I shall be careful," Reginald assured her, "and I shall do my best to accomplish God's work."

"There you are, Vittoria," Alvise said cheerily, placing his arm about her thin shoulders. "Have faith in our Reginald. For if he cannot convince men of reason, who can?"

Vittoria raised her head but did not respond. Reginald smiled at them as he mounted his palfrey. He knew what she was thinking without her speaking the words. She did not believe anyone could bring together the men at Trent. Not even Cardinal Reginald Pole.

~ ~ ~ ~

The city of Trent beckoned from its fertile valley. Two rivers glittered in the distance and the Dolomite Mountains stood sentry over the picturesque scene. Reginald's party descended into the valley, surrounded by spring greenery and the scent of wildflowers. After sneaking down scarcely discernable trails and through dark woods to evade assassins, Trent appeared a welcoming Eden.

As they approached the city, Reginald saw the Church of Santa Maria Maggiore standing tall among the stone buildings. This is where he would make his case for reconciliation and reform. He knew that the Holy Father would not have sent him had he known precisely what Reginald planned to put forward. If the Pope understood Reginald's beliefs that the clergy did, indeed, require reform and that justification was dependent upon faith that spurred on good works . . . well, it was probably just better that he did not know.

December 1545

The months had crept by, the sweltering heat of summer carrying the plague with it. The delegates in Trent had hidden in dark rooms, trying to determine if the sweat on their brow evinced illness or was simply caused by the soaring temperatures. Those who had not arrived before the contagion's advent refused to travel to the city, so those already present had little choice but to wait as the seasons changed.

As tends to occur when sickness attacks a region, the coming of cooler temperatures more effectively defeated the enemy than physicians. By December, the council was finally prepared to begin.

Reginald had avoided the illness, either due to God's protection or his habit of remaining alone in his rented rooms. He was content to write commentaries and letters that he was certain would prove worthier of his time than the results of the eventual council at any rate. He had been able to spend some time with his Cicero, always a balm for his soul.

Cardinal Del Monte was elected to the presidency of the council with little debate or delay. He had used the months of waiting to his advantage, demonstrating his passion for reform and reunification, not to mention his courage in the face of the plague as he daily held audiences with any who were willing to listen for the reward of a place at his luxurious table.

Reginald reflected upon the time he had spent with his fellow cardinal during the slow weeks of restlessness. They were there for God's glory as opposed to their own, were they not? "Of course, of course," Del Monte had replied as he refilled Reginald's goblet with fine French wine.

Del Monte's election bothered Reginald not at all. He was simply energized to finally be beginning the work that he had not wished to be assigned in the first place. He hoped that God would surprise him, that the council would come to monumental agreements on the touchy subjects of clergy reform, authority of scripture, and, of course, justification. Yet, he also confided to himself that he was too cynical to hold much hope.

March 1546

Entering the Santa Maria Maggiore, Reginald felt at home below the soaring limestone held up by pillars in the style of Rome. Only if one looked closely did they notice that the stones could not mimic the comfortably worn appearance of older cathedrals. The walls were startlingly white in their newness, and the sills of the mullioned windows had yet to collect a cushion of dust. An older church had stood upon the site until 1520, but there was no sign of it now.

He strode with purpose to his seat upon a raised platform along one wall. Those of lesser rank had seats in front of the cardinals upon the floor. Reginald was eager to hear which issues Del Monte would introduce first. The reformers were anxious to state their case for clergy reform, while the Pope had let it be known that tenets of faith should take priority. How would the council president keep peace and facilitate debate among parties who could not even agree on what should be discussed?

Reginald's own contribution to this lofty goal had been a sermon given a few weeks earlier. He had been careful to use a conciliatory tone that he hoped had soothed reformers and fellow Catholics alike. As Reginald settled into his chair and waited for others to do the same, he prayed that they see that their objectives – and their God – were the same. Would that the Holy Spirit might descend on these proceedings and lead them to reconciliation.

Gian Pietro Carafa was seated to Reginald's left, and they muttered reluctant greetings in each other's direction. Reginald was well aware that Carafa did not share his hope that the council might bring reunification. The older cardinal glared at the reformers chatting and finding seats throughout the church, making no effort to hide his true feelings.

Reginald withheld a resigned sigh. The hard-headed arrogance was not found only on one side of this debate. He was distracted from Carafa's animosity by Cardinal Cervini taking his place at Reginald's other side. The two exchanged nods of greeting. They were of an age but had not formed a close relationship. Books were Cervini's preferred friends, and Reginald could not much blame him. For when he was sent out to share his great intellect, Cervini was set against impossible opponents such as the horde of Protestants that currently surrounded them.

The deep lines that formed upon Cervini's forehead almost reached the top of his bald head. His full beard kept the true extent of his frown and displeasure from being known. He, too, realizes that our time here is wasted, Reginald thought, and he almost spoke the words aloud. Before a word of complaint could escape his mouth, he clamped it shut, causing Cervini to glance Reginald's way, his frown only slightly lessened.

Finally releasing his captive sigh, Reginald settled into his chair as if he had not intended to say anything at all, a charade Cervini was content to go along with. An image of Alvise came to mind. He always met Reginald's too serious moments with an upraised eyebrow and poorly controlled smirk. It almost made Reginald laugh to realize that he was the cheery, lighthearted one compared to his current company.

This awareness was reasserted at a wedding feast held later in the evening. After a long day of debates where each desired to be heard but none thought to listen, the delegates to Trent were invited to celebrate the marriage of a local couple who would someday tell their doubtful children that no less than four cardinals had attended their wedding.

The food served as a reminder that the area had been decimated by illness, but those in the kitchen had done their best. However, Reginald was tired of sitting and was surprised to discover his own toes tapping as the musicians warmed up instruments and servants removed dinner tables to make room for dancing.

Standing against a wall, where the vibrancy of their red robes seemed to bring light to the dark corner, Reginald and his fellow cardinals watched the local people step and leap in perfect time with each other. Their cheeks turned rosy as sweat beaded at their hairlines, but none seemed to mind. This wedding was more than a celebration of the wedded couple. Everyone there was happy to have escaped the sickness sweeping through the region. They were overjoyed to be alive.

A small area cleared on the dance floor as those couples with the least endurance gave in to their need to refresh themselves. Reginald was unsure who was more surprised, Cervini, Carafa, or himself when Del Monte stepped forward and playfully held a hand out to Reginald.

"Shall we?" he asked, gesturing toward the gyrating crowd with his other hand.

A grin split Reginald's face, making him realize how few times he had smiled since arriving in Trent.

"We shall," he agreed, stepping jauntily to join the dancers.

If the townspeople thought they had a story for their children before, they were outrageously thrilled to see the pious churchmen joining in their dance. They were forgiving when the cardinals took a wrong step or bumped into the person at their side. The rhythm of the dance was happily sacrificed to the novelty of having their special guests join them.

Reginald did not quit the floor until his feet ached and his throat screamed with thirst. He patiently ignored invitations from a few maidens to enjoy more than a dance and made his way toward a table bowed below the weight of wooden barrels of wine and ale. Taking the first cup offered him, careless of its contents, Reginald guzzled half of the wine before he comprehended what it was.

The rest of the evening, he was content to observe. He had created enough of a scandal for the time being. His mood was only slightly deflated by the glare of Carafa, received as the angry cardinal swept from the hall in a state of righteous fury.

A few days later, the council received word that Martin Luther, arguably the reason they were all gathered here, had died. Would that make the reformers more or less open to reconciliation, Reginald wondered. Sniffles and coughing echoing through the cathedral served as reminders that the sickness that had so long delayed the opening of the council continued to threaten those who attended.

More than ever, Reginald wished to be recalled to Rome.

June 1546

A breeze collecting coolness from the nearby mountaintops battled with the searing summer sun for dominance in Reginald's borrowed rooms. His body seemed incapable of regulating the temperature between these two forces. The stir of wind would raise goosebumps on his flesh, but a moment standing near the window to soak up warmth of the sun made sweat bead on his brow.

A knock at the door caused him to turn from the window, and a petite, but solidly built, woman entered with a fresh pitcher of water and linen cloths. She took one glance at the churchman, and, though she had not dared to speak to him before, she moved toward him.

"Are you feeling quite well?" she asked, fear and wonder mingling in her voice.

Reginald only blinked at her, his eyes dilating and vision blurring with the effort. He had been trying to deny it, of course, but the illness that had ravaged the countryside had found him. He had one last thought before crashing to the floor at the feet of the stunned servant. How satisfied Henry of England would be to hear of his demise.

~ ~ ~ ~

A droning voice brought Reginald out of the darkness, although he had no clue how much time had passed. As he struggled to bring the room into focus, he realized two things. Night had fallen, and the voice belonged to Cardinal Del Monte.

He was reciting news of the day as though packing it away in his memory. Reginald heard mirrored in Del Monte's voice his own frustration that the council was failing in each objective set before it. He was not able to catch every word, but the name Betoun stood out when agonizingly uttered.

Cardinal Betoun had also been the target for King Henry's

assassins. Only a few weeks earlier, they had been successful. Was Del Monte afraid of losing Reginald as well?

Though the thought was touching, Reginald could not focus upon it for long. He felt his consciousness fading as Del Monte's voice droned on.

When Reginald next awoke, the only thing he knew was that he was ravenously hungry. Brightness filled his room, and he wondered if more than one night had passed and how long Del Monte had kept him company in his delirious state. It was greater compassion and caring than he would have expected of the ambitious cardinal, yet he was thankful for it.

Moving his eyes about the room, he did not find anyone to beg of a drink and piece of bread. Reginald suspected that his voice would have the volume of a church mouse rather than an orator were he to attempt to call for someone, so he waited patiently until the woman he had collapsed before reentered the room.

How many times had she come as he lay sleeping, he wondered. She moved about the room in comfort and with purpose, not glancing at him long enough to realize that she was observed. He cleared his throat to gain her attention without startling her, and she quickly approached his bedside.

"Cardinal Pole," she stated, taking an inventory of his color and temperature. Seeming content with his condition, she asked, "Would you like to try a bite to eat?"

"I would," he replied appreciatively. He tried to raise his left arm in thanks but was surprised that it remained heavy atop the bedcoverings. Reginald frowned at his hand, concentrating on flexing the fingers. They moved, but not into the strong grip he willed them into.

"Don't you tire yourself out now," the woman urged, taking up his hand and rubbing warmth into it. "You will find that your strength restores in time."

With that lack of concern, she exited the room in search of warm broth for her patient. Reginald's eyes remained on his disobedient hand. At the same time, he realized he was twisting his neck at an awkward angle to glare in that direction because the vision in his left eye was gone.

After a few days, much of Reginald's health had returned, but his left side remained handicapped. He could use his arm, but it lacked its former strength. The vision in his left eye was only somewhat restored, and he wondered if reading and writing would now be difficult.

His belongings had been capably packed up by the same woman who had cared for him over the two weeks of his illness. The trunks were piled into a wagon pulled by stocky horses as a litter was prepared for Reginald. He did not remember ever before traveling in one of the contraptions that he felt were for royalty, women, or old men. He supposed he knew which of those he now was.

"You will return to us?" the voice held a note of pleading, yet Reginald still recognized it from his sickroom.

"I do not know, Giovanni," Reginald admitted to Cardinal Del Monte. Reginald felt guilty leaving him there with the vicious Carafa and quiet Cervini, but he was helpless to do more. "I am no longer certain what God has in store for me."

Del Monte appeared to wish to argue. He needed Reginald at the Council if he had any hope for success. However, as he evaluated Reginald's appearance, he knew that he was asking too much.

"I shall pray for your prompt and complete healing," he said instead.

Reginald only nodded before accepting the help of his attendants to be settled in the litter. He prayed for his healing as well. If not to be made whole again, to at least be restored to a condition in which he could be useful.

It took their slow procession twice as long as normal to make their way to Padua, where Reginald could convalesce at the home of Cardinal Bembo. It had been determined by others, much to Reginald's dismay, that to travel all the way to Viterbo was out of the question in his current condition.

If he had to choose anywhere other than Viterbo to recuperate, Reginald could be happy in Padua, where he had spent happy days as a young student, in the company of one of his greatest and oldest friends.

Seeing the town appear upon the horizon, Reginald could finally smile. He may be an invalid – possibly would be for the rest of his life – but he was in one of the few places on Earth he considered home.

~ ~ ~ ~

Reginald was surprised by a visit from Cardinal Carafa a fortnight later. He had been spending his days in edifying conversation and exercises he hoped would return strength to his left arm. The relationship between he and Carafa had once been friendlier than it had become due to their difference in opinion on how to deal with reformers, but it never had been close enough to justify sickbed visits.

Therefore, Reginald knew that Carafa was spying on him, only he did not know why. Since he had nothing to hide, he welcomed the fierce, grey-bearded man as if the visit pleased him very much indeed.

"It is very kind of you to come," Reginald said, gesturing Carafa to a comfortable chair. "Bembo and I have not had many visitors. People are too busy or to afraid of illness, I suppose."

"So, there has been sickness here?" Carafa inquired doubtfully.

He had not taken long to get right to the heart of the matter.

Reginald realized that Carafa thought he was feigning illness, and it only took another moment to realize why.

"I have been slowly improving," Reginald said. He would not be goaded into saying anything that the crafty cardinal might use against him.

Carafa raised a bushy eyebrow and pierced him with his gaze. "How lucky for you, in the end," he sighed dramatically. "Your illness forced you to leave the council just when we were getting to the vital discussion of justification."

"That is unfortunate," Reginald said, praying that his voice would not break. Carafa had pressed Pope Paul to give him charge of an inquisition, and now Reginald realized that was why he was here. "The question of justification is one of the most important dividing us from our brothers and sisters in Christ," Reginald stated more firmly.

Carafa pretended to be surprised. "The heretics need only embrace the truth as it has been handed down to us through the centuries. How could one lowly monk understand justification better than our long line of learned popes? They receive their position and wisdom from God himself."

Reginald bowed his head in acceptance of this statement, not daring to respond.

"We should be arresting and punishing these heretics before they can lead more people astray," Carafa continued, the passion in his voice rising with each word.

"What of winning them back to the true faith?" Reginald asked.

Carafa wearily waved the idea away. "Not those such as the men at Trent. They have made their choice. Now it is our duty to protect any they might influence. Instead of negotiating with them, we should be tying them to the stake!"

"You would burn them?" Reginald blurted, too shocked to

restrain his words.

Carafa leaned close enough for Reginald to smell the wine on his breath before whispering a warning, "Even if my own father were a heretic, I would gather the wood to burn him."

Calmly leaning away from his fellow cardinal, Reginald expertly kept his fear and revulsion from his features. He let the silence lengthen. It was a skill of his to not feel pressured to be the one to break it. His gaze remained on the face of this man who seemed filled with an unexplainable amount of hatred – too much for a man of God.

When he realized that Reginald was not going to respond, Carafa also slowly leaned back and took up his wine. He commented on its vintage, then on the weather.

After his visitor had left, Reginald reflected upon this strange interlude. It seemed almost of a dream quality, and he wondered if he had truly just been threatened by the Inquisitor General.

November 1546

When the time came for Reginald to leave Bembo's comfortable estate in Padua, it was with mixed feelings that he packed his belongings. The months spent with Pietro had been revitalizing in mind and body, aside from Carafa's disturbing interruption. Some strength had been regained in Reginald's left side, and he was certain that no one who was unaware of his ailment would be able to observe it. More than that, the hours spent in enriching discussion had lifted Reginald's spirits and reminded him why he had dedicated his life to study and faith.

Yet, Reginald had duties needing his attention. He would not be returning to Trent, for Pope Paul required his assistance in Rome. News had reached him that the King of England was in failing health. Could the time be coming when Reginald could return to his homeland?

With a start, Reginald realized that he did not truly consider England his home. He may have been born there, but he had spent much more time, and agreeable time at that, in vibrant Italy. He would go wherever he was called. For now, that meant Rome.

He did wish for some time in Viterbo and hoped to pass there on the way to Rome. News of Vittoria's failing health concerned him, and he had been away for far too long. His recuperation had forced him to focus on prayer as the only way he was able to be of service to those he cared for.

The last of his trunks closed and locked, Reginald cast his eyes around the comfortable rooms that Bembo had loaned to him these several months. As pleasant as they were, it was time for him to return to his work.

Reginald watched servants hoist heavy burdens onto their backs and stow them within wagons of the caravan that would take him to Viterbo. With some jealousy of their strength and good health, he followed at a slow easy pace, trying not to too much favor his left leg.

"Do let Vittoria know that I pray fervently for her," Bembo requested, holding Reginald's hand in a fierce grip. "She is the finest woman poet of our day."

"She will be honored to know you said so," Reginald said with a smile. "Her verse is humble and rather not worth sharing in her own opinion."

With a laugh, Bembo declared, "Well, women have been known to be occasionally wrong. But only occasionally!"

"She rarely is," Reginald agreed, wishing that Bembo was returning to Viterbo and Rome with him. "You have been a steadfast friend. Thank you," he said as he prepared to mount his horse. He had insisted upon riding as long as he was physically capable. He refused to be treated as an invalid.

"You act as though we will never see each other again," Bembo observed with a searching gaze. "Have you had a premonition."

"Nothing as profound as that," Reginald assured him. "I will just miss your company, my dear friend."

"And I yours," Bembo agreed, shaking Reginald's hand ever more heartily. "And I yours. Now travel safely and be well until we see each other again."

Dipping his head in acknowledgement, Reginald joined his caravan and took the road heading south toward Rome.

January 1547

Reginald had ignored pleas for him to return to Trent, primarily due to his health but secretly because he no longer wished to be a part of it. He had held on to his noble hopes for unification, especially on the vital issue of justification. However, the attitudes that he had encountered on both sides had crushed his spirits and made him long for isolated meditation. And he could not forget Carafa's icy glare as he had pledged willingness to burn even his own father for heretical beliefs.

Since leaving the council, Reginald had enjoyed several months of relative isolation during the long healing process, but a desire to rejoin his fellow cardinals in Trent had not sparked. He preferred Padua with Pietro or Viterbo and the company of Alvise and Vittoria. Reginald had been troubled to find Vittoria ailing when he had finally returned home. She, of course, had implied that her illness was of no consequence in her correspondence, but she could not hide the fact that she had grown frail during his absence.

"You would not believe it to see me now," she had reminisced as she waved away his concerns, "but I once danced so elegantly for Sigismund of Poland that news of the evening was spoken of throughout the region."

Reginald smiled fondly and took up her small, withered hand. "It is not so difficult to imagine," he assured her, and the wrinkles at the corners of her eyes deepened in pleasure. "How disappointed the young men must have been to discover that you were also a pious scholar."

A bark of laughter escaped Vittoria's dry lips at that. "You are well acquainted with men's expectations of women for a priest!" she teased.

"Ah, I am not a priest, but a cardinal," Reginald reminded her of the minor difference. "Were God to lead me, I could yet leave my position and take a wife. Had I only discovered you when we were younger," he added with a wink that caused Vittoria to cackle loudly once again.

"I have always been too old for you," she protested, though the sparkle did not leave her eyes. "Maybe God has a royal wife in mind for you."

Reginald knew that she referred to his cousin, Princess Mary of England. She was more than ten years younger than he, but that was no obstacle. No, the complication between them, had they wished to wed, was her father. "King Henry would never allow it," Reginald pointed out, not for the first time. "If he did not wish the match when my mother was still the close confidant of his adored queen, he certainly will not see it done now that he wishes me dead."

"Someday, the girl will be without her father's iron fist posed above her. Then, perhaps, she will call upon you."

"Perhaps," Reginald agreed casually. He saw no future for himself as a husband, let alone to a royal princess, regardless of whether her father now called her a bastard. His mother had loved the girl just as much as her own children . . . . but he would not think of that just now.

Vittoria seemed contented with his acquiescence, for she leaned back against soft pillows and closed her eyes as the setting sun blanketed the room with a soft golden glow. Reginald whispered a short prayer before letting himself out of her rooms.

Upon returning to his home, he was surprised to see the horses and wagons of a visiting party in the courtyard. Although he was not expecting anyone, he could not have been more shocked by who his guest turned out to be.

"Pietro!" Reginald exclaimed as he found Cardinal Bembo reclined on a couch that had been placed in a corner of the garden where evening sun continued to offer warmth. "You should not have attempted such a trip!"

"At my age, you mean," added Pietro sardonically.

"I only care for your health, my friend," Reginald said without apology. "You yourself said the travel was a burden for you."

"So, I did. So, I did," Bembo agreed. "Yet, I am called to Rome, so it is to Rome I must go."

Bembo lifted one hand as if he would reach out to take Reginald's and pat it to emphasize his words, but his strength failed him, and his arm wearily fell to his side. At that moment, Alvise entered the garden.

"Please, see to it that..." Reginald began, but he was cut off by Alvise's upheld hand.

"The best of your wine and most comforting of food has been ordered up for our dear cardinal," Alvise assured him with a tip of his head. "The bedroom that enjoys the most morning sun is currently being prepared for his rest."

Reginald thanked him without taking his eyes off Pietro. He appeared frailer even than when he had last seen him. Why would the Pope insist upon his travel? Then, shaking his head, he silently reprimanded himself. It was not his place to judge the decisions of Christ's appointed.

The next day, Bembo departed looking no better rested than he had on arrival. Reginald had begged him to stay, but duty could not be evaded. The caravan crept out of Viterbo in the light of a pale morning sun.

Time at prayer gave Reginald some peace before he checked on Vittoria's condition. She was no better but no worse, and Reginald hoped that this might prove to be only a minor setback for her. She had endured much in her lifetime, and he was certain she could see this through.

The next day, word reached him that Cardinal Bembo was

dead. Tears rolled down Reginald's cheeks as he wondered how he could ever forgive himself for allowing the old man to leave.

~ ~ ~ ~

Reginald had not wished to give Vittoria the news of Bembo's death, but he was unable to keep the grief from his features during his visits. The two had long been friends, brought together by their mutual love of poetry, yet Vittoria took the news of his passing with dignified peace.

"I shall see him soon, and neither of us will be housed within shriveled up old bodies any longer," she said when Reginald examined her for signs of a dramatic, womanly breakdown.

He could manage only a thin smile. "Indeed, you will."

February 1547

News of another death reached them within weeks of Bembo's passing. Reginald would not have admitted aloud that this death did not sadden him the way it should have. The way the death of the aging cardinal had.

"King Henry of England has died," he shared with Vittoria only moments after receiving the news himself.

She was now bedridden, and neither of them admitted that she was unlikely to ever rise from the luxurious bed that Reginald had provided her with.

"We should pray for his soul," Vittoria insisted. "No man was ever in so much fear and doubt of heaven as he, yet God desires that all should be saved."

Without further discussion of the final destination of the Head of the Church of England, Reginald bowed his head with Vittoria and prayed fervently for the man who had murdered his brother and mother.

He knew not how much time had passed before he arose and strolled slowly to his study. How strange, he thought, that he could now move freely without fear of assassins. Stranger still that he had become so accustomed to the constant threat that it almost felt as if he had lost something.

Reginald took his time, appreciating the beauty of Viterbo as one does after the realization that another has gone on to a world where they will no longer enjoy earthly surroundings. Once he finally settled himself behind his sturdy but simple desk, he composed a letter. In it, Reginald offered his services to privy council of King Edward VI.

It was completed and mailed before Reginald could consider second thoughts. While England no longer felt like home to him, he felt it was appropriate for him to let Henry's son know that he could count him as a friend.

Wishing to share what he had done with Vittoria, though certain she would approve, Reginald again found himself on the cobblestone streets of Viterbo. He was thinking that he would ask her to once again tell him of the time she met Niccolo Machiavelli when Vittoria's closest servant stopped him at her door.

He looked at her curiously, having never been turned away before. Then he noticed the blotchy, red spots covering her face but heaviest around her eyes. Her hands trembled as she held them out to force him to pause. His heart dropped as she struggled to form words that neither of them desired to hear.

"She has gone to God?" Reginald whispered.

The poor woman could only nod her head before breaking into uncontrollable sobbing. Reginald rested his hand lightly on her shoulder, looking over her head so that she would not feel ashamed of her outburst.

"She is the happiest of we three," he whispered just loud enough for her to hear. "We continue to bear this world's burdens, while Vittoria is experiencing the unimaginable joy of heaven in the presence of her Savior."

"Of course," Vittoria's woman sniffled. Reginald could see that she attempted to compose herself for his sake.

"There is no shame in grief," he said, looking into her bloodshot eyes. "Yet, we have hope that death cannot trample. Keep that in mind – until you see her again."

Then he turned and slowly retraced his steps, feeling that Fortune's Wheel had scraped bottom and wondering if it would ever ascend for him again.

January 1548 - September 1549

Scattered papers covered the desktop in apparent disorder, but Reginald knew what was written on each sheet. Whenever he picked one up to read or move to reach one beneath it, he did it with utmost care. The author of these works could no longer reproduce them.

Bembo's verse both comforted and grieved Reginald. It was a joy to immerse himself in the skillful prose, but the constant reminder of his friend left a deep hole in his heart. It did no good to turn away and explore his shelves, for they, too, held bound volumes written by both Pietro and Vittoria.

She had forged a pathway for the woman poets of Italy. Reginald sighed and wondered if she knew. Several talented ladies had published books of poetry since Vittoria's passing in the hope of filling the space she left behind, but, for Reginald at least, it was a vain hope.

Death always causes the mourner to consider his own mortality, but this did not bother Reginald in the least. Heaven seemed almost closer to him than earth, and he longed to join the many waiting to greet him there. However, he also refused to be fatalistic. As long as he was alive, God gave him work and he would see it done.

After taking a moment to stretch, he began eagerly scanning Bembo's writing again, as if seeing it for the first time.

An unknown amount of time had passed when a middle-aged woman brought in a tray. Reginald was surprised to discover that he was hungry, and he wondered who had thought to ensure that he took sustenance as he thanked the servant.

She had also brought in correspondence, so he perused it with one hand while holding a thick slice of bread in the other. A missive bearing the Duke of Somerset's seal caused him to, once again, forget about food. After he had read it, he had even more reason to wish that his friends were still with him, for he found himself desperately in need of their counsel.

Edward Seymour, uncle of England's young king, had offered Reginald a passport – safe passage to the home that had been denied to him these many years. Home? Reginald slouched back in his chair. The weariness and emotion of the day caused his left hand to shake and the letter fell from his grasp.

He did not immediately reach to retrieve it. The words were already emblazoned on his mind. Did he think of England as home? Did he wish to return? Could he trust Somerset that he would be safe?

He had too many questions, so Reginald took them where he always did. As he slowly stood and left his study for the chapel, the Duke of Somerset's letter was lifted slightly by the breeze of the door and skidded across the floor.

Reginald did not often prostrate himself upon the floor before the altar as he had preferred to do when he was younger, when he had not been concerned regarding his ability to rise again with dignity. Instead, he knelt upon a cushion and bowed deeply over the railing. With his world in turmoil, he was experiencing difficulty in discerning God's will.

Should he return to England now that those closest to him in Italy were gone? Before he had completed the thought, another countered it. All he had been close to in England were gone as well.

Could he advise the new king? Edward was already known to be even more of a reformer than his father, but he was young and might be steered aright by a skilled teacher.

Rather than try to answer his own questions, Reginald forced his mind to clear and whispered, "God, speak to me. I am listening."

~ ~ ~ ~

Correspondence with the Duke of Somerset had been

ongoing, but Reginald was no clearer on whether he should offer his services to Edward's privy council or remain in Viterbo. The Pope clarified his calling when he made a routine trip to Rome.

"No good can come of you sacrificing yourself to that heathen land," Pope Paul exclaimed. "They have executed the king's own uncle! Safe passage indeed!" Reginald wondered if the passionate response was because Paul did not wish to lose Reginald's services or if he truly believed England was a land beyond hope.

"It is a waste of your time to consider it," Paul said with finality before Reginald had formed a response. Seeing that his cardinal prepared to continue the conversation, he changed the subject entirely, "I have a mind to make you Bishop of Spoleti."

With an almost audible gasp, Reginald stepped back from the Pope and peered at him through narrowed eyes. Tilting his head in observation, Reginald wondered, for the first time, if Alessandro Farnese was interpreting God's will for them all or delegating out his own.

Declining both the bishopric and position on the privy council of the King of England, Reginald returned to Viterbo.

November 1549

Within a matter of months, Reginald's position became more unclear than ever. He was busying himself with Bembo's writing in the hope that he would publish a comprehensive volume of his scholarly work when a breathless servant rushed into his study.

His raised eyebrows were the only reprimand before the young woman exclaimed in an unsteady rush, "A messenger, from Rome."

A quick stride brought Reginald to the hall where he realized the reason for the servant's panic. Messengers from Rome arrived with frequency, but this was a full guard of papal troops, elaborately decorated to create just that type of awe and fear in those who saw them. Reginald, however, was unintimidated.

"Who is in charge here?" he bellowed, causing all heads to turn in his direction, but none stepped forward. "I am Cardinal Pole. Who is it that requests an audience with me?"

Then a man did approach him, but later Reginald could never remember who he had been or what exactly he had said. All that remained, stamped inexorably on his mind was the core of his message. Pope Paul was dead. All of the cardinals were called to Rome for a conclave to elect their next leader.

December 1549

Riding into Rome, Reginald reflected upon how the city had changed since he had first arrived more than two decades earlier. Gone was the detritus that had clogged the streets, and new structures had risen from the ruins that had made Rome appear much less spectacular than he had been expecting as a young man.

Even the Vatican was reformed with Bramante's basilica prominently rising where the ancient St Peter's had stood. Reginald shook his head in renewed astonishment that the aged Michelangelo now served as chief architect on the project, and Reginald wondered if either of them would be blessed to see it completed.

Casting off his meanderings, Reginald forced his mind to focus on the task at hand. Time to grieve would have to come later, for now was the time to select a new leader. How could the college of cardinals determine who God had chosen to be his representative on earth? He felt entirely inadequate to the task.

Directing his feet toward the Pauline Chapel, Reginald felt some joy rise in his chest as he realized this was his opportunity to see the frescoes only recently completed by Michelangelo. Had Pope Paul observed the final work before experiencing the glory of heaven? Reginald understood his friend's faith and art well enough to anticipate a breathtaking scene as a setting for the conclave.

The Sistine Chapel, where Michelangelo had labored for years to complete the ceiling that he trusted to no assistant's brush, had been split into small, temporary cells for the cardinals. Men who were used to living in luxury were encouraged to hurry along their decision by the uncomfortable quarters. Reginald claimed his before hurrying along to the Pauline Chapel.

The sounds of raised voices in heated argument drowned out the sound of his footsteps long before he entered the room. Closing his eyes to grasp one last moment of peace before entering,

Reginald sighed and moved forward.

The cacophony faded away as his eyes were drawn to the wall to the left of the doorway he had just passed through. Suddenly, it was as though Reginald and the apostle Paul were the only ones in the room. The sun shone on from a high window directly onto the painting, making it appear that the lightening striking the road in front of Paul had truly come down from heaven and into the chapel. Although he had seen the work in progress, Reginald's eyes were almost as wide as the onlookers in the painting upon seeing the final work. No wonder Saul bowed low before the voice of God and took on his new, apostolic name.

Michelangelo had captured the terror, amazement, and confusion in the faces of the figures traveling with Saul on the road to Damascus. How many had believed him and converted themselves? Which became his persecutors? The fresco almost moved with life.

Reginald was uncertain how long he stood before his friend's masterpiece before the voices invaded and his attention was dragged away from the heavenly encounter.

Alvise had a hand on his arm. "Reginald, you are certain to be elected. I will consider it a great privilege to have been your friend."

Reginald's jaw fell open and all thoughts of the apostle Paul fled his mind. He scrutinized his friend's face for signs of mirth but found only sincere devotion.

"Who has been saying this?" he demanded. "I have not put myself forward."

"Everyone," Alvise said with a shrug, holding his hands out to encompass the entire gathering of churchmen. "The Florentine bankers have extraordinarily high odds on you."

Shaking his head, Reginald tried to take this in on top of everything crowded in his mind. "How?" he asked absently.

"You are admired for your learnedness and trusted as one who denies himself some of the luxuries that our fellow cardinals indulge in. Choosing you pleases his grace the Holy Roman Emperor, because it leaves the Lady Mary available for him to control. You are an ideal compromise, if not everyone's first choice."

"It is to be God's choice!" Reginald cried. Seeing too many eyes turning his way, he took a deep breath, lowered his voice, and leaned toward Alvise. "I did not hope for this and will not scheme for it."

"Of course not!" Alvise agreed as if offended.

"I should thank you," Reginald continued more calmly. "You have taken me by surprise, but no one else shall. When is the first scrutiny?"

"As soon as possible. It should have occurred already. Only waiting on those traveling from France has held the vote off this long."

Alvise gave a shallow bow before walking away, and nobody else approached. Reginald examined the crowd, looking for kindness or animosity in the eyes that covertly sought him out. He missed Bembo's greeting upon arrival, missed his friendship that would have comforted him in this moment.

Taking one last glance at Paul, kneeling in the road in repentance, Reginald turned and left the chapel.

~ ~ ~ ~

When Reginald next entered the Pauline Chapel, he thought he might leave it as Rome's next pope. He had spent a restless night in his comfortless cubicle, wondering what outcome he hoped for and praying that God's will would be done.

On his previous visit, he had only had time to examine one of Michelangelo's frescoes. Now, as he took his seat amid the senior cardinals, he came face to face with the other.

A wave of contrition overcame Reginald, and he felt the burden of every sin he had ever committed, as the eyes of Saint Peter bore into him from his place on the cross. Unlike the crucifixion of our Savior, Peter was upside-down. The pain would have been unbearable, but not so much that the fiery disciple could not turn his head to glare at the unworthy who filled the chapel.

Could Reginald bear such a fate? He had sacrificed much in the service of his God. His entire family had. Yet, as he averted his eyes from Peter's intense gaze, his contemptibility was upon him with heavy force.

He wondered how the others seemed unaffected by the scenes that Michelangelo had brought to life in this dark, awkward chapel. The poor light had been utilized for dramatic impact, and the subjects seemed to be chosen for the conviction that the artist hoped the gathered cardinals would feel. As Reginald took his seat, he was both drawn to the fresco and had a desire to avoid so much as another glimpse.

Little conversation took place before the slips of paper were passed around. All the negotiating and convincing had gone on in secret, in little groups huddled together in corners and alcoves, as they had waited for the necessary participants to arrive. It came down to this moment and a few characters scratched upon an insignificant scrap.

Reginald could not stop himself from looking around the room, wondering how many would have his name written upon them. Then he forced his gaze down to the blank sheet in front of him and asked God to tell him what he should write there.

The moments passed in silence, each cardinal placing their vote in a gaudily decorated box before shuffling back to their seat to await the outcome. When each paper had been inscribed, folded twice, and submitted, the scrutineer took up the box and opened it with reverent movements. The collective breath of the room was held as he picked up the first name.

"Reginald Pole."

It was a profound feeling to hear his own name ringing out to break the thick silence.

And then it did again.

And again.

Then Cardinal Cervini's name was read, and a few people started breathing again.

Forty-one times the scrutineer slowly unfolded a paper, read a name, and then impaled the slip on a needle to place it on a thread that held all the counted votes. Twenty-seven votes were required for a winner to be declared.

Reginald had received twenty-six.

He strode from the chapel quickly, not knowing if he was disappointed or relieved, but certain that he did not wish to be accosted by those seeking his response. Alone in his tiny partitioned space, he knelt. He did not pray, not even silently. Instead, he opened himself up to listen and hoped that God would speak.

Before any divine message had the chance to arrive, Alvise interrupted Reginald's devotion. As Reginald stood, others followed Alvise, filling the inadequate space.

"Do not be dismayed, my friend," Alvise began. He continued without giving Reginald an opportunity to insist that he was not. "We still wish to do this tonight."

"Whatever do you mean?" Reginald asked. The lines of his face deepened. He did not like the sound of this.

"By adoration," a voice, not Alvise's, insisted. "The Holy Spirit moves us to declare you our Holy Father. Now. Tonight."

"The papal robes are being tailored for you as we speak," Alvise added. He seemed to hope he was lightening the mood, but the news distressed Reginald.

"This great office is more to be feared than desired. If it is

God's will that it should come to me, I will not have it said that I acquired it through duplicitous means. If you wish to support my election, please do so tomorrow – with your vote. I will not participate in secret, midnight declarations."

At least one voice was raised in protest, but Alvise quieted it and herded the men from the room. Reginald returned to his knees. He would sacrifice a night of sleep for the comfort of prayer.

~ ~ ~ ~

A fortnight later, Reginald wondered if he had made the right decision. Although they had held fifteen scrutinies, the college of cardinals had failed to elect the next pope. As more cardinals arrived, the voting became more fractured with some names receiving a dozen votes in one scrutiny only to be replaced by another candidate in the next. Reginald received between twenty-two and twenty-six each time, but with more cardinals continuously arriving a greater number was needed to reach the required two-thirds majority.

As Christmas approached, they seemed to be at an impasse, and Reginald wondered if he had made a mistake when he declined the efforts of his greatest supporters that first night. The increasingly cramped rooms partitioned in the Sistine Chapel were becoming unhealthy with debris piling up and illness trapped within the walls. Sneezing and hacking were heard throughout the night as the black smoke hung heavy above the Vatican.

January 1550

The charcoal fires burning in the chapel made Reginald's head spin, and he wondered if they were releasing some poison into the air that did not occur when wood was burned. The atmosphere was stifling. Fresh air seemed like something out of a distant dream. He was no longer certain he cared who was elected, but only longed to be released from this miasmic prison.

Imperial and French factions schemed for supremacy, yet there were enough cardinals who were not part of either that the votes continued to be hopelessly split. A new candidate, Cardinal Alvarez was put forward as a compromise. He would be better than Carafa, Reginald thought, forgetting for a moment that it was supposed to be God choosing the very best man for the job rather than men politicking for authority.

Cardinal Ridolphi had been receiving a handful of votes in the last few scrutinies. Reginald was no longer certain exactly how many they had held. However, about midmonth, the poor man was carried from his cell wailing in anguish. Feeling certain that Ridolphi would recover quickly once away from the ill air inside, Reginald was almost jealous of his ailment.

Then news arrived that Ridolphi was dead. It was whispered that he had been poisoned by more than malodorous air, and Reginald was dismayed by his own lack of shock.

This was not the way it was supposed to be. How could they hope to elect God's anointed this way? In the midst of Reginald's personal introspection, Alvise arrived, looking thinner and paler than Reginald could remember seeing him.

"Are you feeling alright," Alvise asked him by way of greeting.

"As well as anyone in this pit. Pray that God soon releases us from our duties here that we may return to the sweet air of Viterbo."

"Amen," Alvise agreed enthusiastically. He leaned in closer, making it clear that he had more serious discussion in mind than their poor living conditions. "Reg, the right words in the right ears, and you can end this. Possibly today. Certainly tomorrow."

Reginald's head shook back and forth before the words were complete. "I will not campaign for a position that is only God's to give. I will not make promises and bargains to achieve the highest office on earth. One lesson I learned from my late cousin is that you should never attempt to steal power that rightly belongs to God alone."

Alvise sighed. His shoulders slumped. "You could be pope," he insisted. "If only you would speak for yourself."

Reginald smiled. "There is no need for me to do so when I have good friends like you to make my case and God to guide the hands of those voting."

"You must at least respond to Carafa's charges!"

"Are you afraid that our fellow cardinals believe me a heretic, Alvise?"

"No. Not most of them," Alvise agreed, but held a hand up before Reginald could consider the matter closed. "They do not all know you as well as I do. You no longer have Bembo to speak for you among the more senior members of the conclave. Some only know what they have been told by their enemies."

"You must accept, as I have," Reginald calmly stated, "that the Lord might not require this of me."

Shaking his head doubtfully, Alvise did not push him further. While others bribed and blackmailed behind the scenes, Reginald serenely prayed. Alivse suspected it would not be a winning strategy.

February 1550

White smoke had finally soared above the Vatican and dissipated over the city of Rome. Cheers rang out once those on the street realized what it meant. Inside the Sistine Chapel, where temporary walls were already being torn down, Reginald searched his heart. Had he made a mistake?

The coronation of Pope Julius III was planned for later in the month, and Reginald would kneel to kiss the foot of Giovanni Del Monte who had finally triumphed as an acceptable compromise candidate. Had God chosen him instead of Reginald, or had Reginald failed to grasp the opportunity that had been placed directly in front of him?

It did not matter. The weeks flew by in a whirlwind of preparations, during which Reginald attempted to keep himself from thinking about the papal robes that had been tailored just for him. Would new ones be sewn for the man he must now think of as Julius or would those intended for him be refitted?

Reginald was not involved in the coronation plans. He preferred to lock himself away with his latest writing, a document on the nature of the supreme office that he had begun when he thought to fill that position. The work had settled and centered him between scrutinies and it served that same purpose now.

He was not interested in the rumors floating around, even cardinals were not immune to the lure of the gossip mill. None of it mattered. The conclave was over.

~ ~ ~ ~

Pope Julius III sat upon the papal throne as the college of cardinals sang the coronation mass. Deep, resounding voices rose up to God, at least as Michelangelo had depicted him in the peak of the Sistine Chapel. The ostentatious tiara was carefully balanced upon the new pope's head, and Reginald could perceive that Julius was focusing upon keeping it steady.

For Reginald's part, he was concentrating on remaining humble, trying not to second guess his actions, and demonstrating thankfulness to God that they had a new leader and that it was not him. He felt that he had succeeded in these goals until the moment came for the cardinals to give Julius their obeisance. Forcing away the feeling of humiliation that Satan sent to plague him, Reginald bowed low before his former colleague and prepared to kiss his foot.

He almost gasped when a hand stopped him before he could complete the ritual. Glancing up, Reginald encountered understanding and respect in Giovanni's eyes.

"Holy Father," Reginald whispered as he began to bend again toward the floor.

"No, my son. It is not desired or needful of you," Giovanni, now Julius, whispered in return before embracing Reginald in the view of all of those who had been plotting to gain their own desires from the conclave. "I will be depending upon you a great deal."

The words were in Reginald's ear where no one else could overhear them. As they embraced, Reginald remembered them dancing together at the wedding in Trent. Del Monte was a good choice, whether the cardinals' or God's, he thought. Then Julius released Reginald and the solemn ceremony continued as if nothing amiss had occurred.

June 1550

Reginald had returned to Viterbo as soon as politeness allowed. He held no grudge against Del Monte, but he did have matters to attend to, especially since the term of his legation was almost at an end.

He would miss Viterbo and knew not yet what duties the new pope would assign him. It was only when he had returned to the place that felt most like home to him at this point in his life that he heard what he had refused to listen to during the conclave.

"Carafa not only accused you of heresy," Alvise seemed only too glad to inform him, "he claimed that you had a bastard daughter housed in Viterbo's convent."

Unable to control his reaction to this news, Reginald's eyebrows shot upward. Yet, he was surprised by the relief that flowed through him.

"I am thankful, then, that Carafa did not succeed in buying the election. God's will has been done."

Now it was Alvise's turn to be shocked. "You do not regret refusing to campaign?"

"I do not, for I am certain that Our Lord has other plans for me. I am his willing servant."

Alvise shook his head in astonishment. "One cannot argue with a saint," he muttered. Louder, he asked, "Will you at least publish a response to the accusations – clear your name?"

Reginald settled deeper into his chair to consider this question. He felt certain that a response would only give the rumors greater hold and that anyone who knew him well would not believe them anyway. No, lies were not the reason he had failed to achieve the highest office. He was needed somewhere else.

But, to appease Alvise, he said, "I will think on it."

It would have to be enough.

~ ~ ~ ~

His legation to Viterbo over, Reginald returned to Rome once more, full of hope and anticipation. What was the future that God had reserved for him?

He did not have to wait long to find out.

"I have created a committee for church reform," Julius informed him. "You and five others, whom I trust implicitly to manage such a serious task, will investigate what is necessary for redeeming the reputation of our Holy Mother Church."

Reginald could not help but think that practices such as Julius raising his own nephew to cardinal was an example of actions that should be abolished, but he accepted the role with humility. He was preparing to leave the pope's presence when Julius cleared his throat.

"I know that you are privy to things that were said . . ." he trailed off, uncertain of his course. "Things that should not have been said . . ."

"We do not need to speak of it," Reginald insisted, not wishing to share in his friend's embarrassment.

"But we do," Julius said with greater confidence in his voice. "I must beg your forgiveness."

"It is yours."

Reginald once again prepared to bow and leave, but Julius stopped him again.

"I know that you are encouraged to publish a defense." He paused, clearly not relishing the words he seemed to feel he must say anyway. "I would ask you not to write such a thing."

Tilting his head almost imperceptibly to the side, Reginald considered this appeal. He truly had no intention of publishing a defense, but it was intriguing that Julius felt strongly enough about it to make such a request. After a moment, during which a single drip of sweat ran down the pope's face, Reginald acquiesced.

He tipped his head toward Julius and promised, "Nothing of the sort will come from my pen."

July 1553

Three years passed, and Reginald was beginning to wonder, not for the first time, if he had made a mistake. None of the tasks assigned to him since the conclave of 1550 seemed significant enough to warrant his failure to gain the papal tiara. He had strived to serve the church to the best of his ability, recommending reforms, participating in councils, making attempts at reconciliation with Protestants.

But three years had passed, and none of it was enough. He was capable of a greater calling and was getting impatient to learn what it might be.

Then a packet arrived from England. Not a simple letter, but a heavy bundle of them, as if everyone in his homeland was eager to be the first to give him important news.

He had rarely received letters from England since the death of Edward Seymour. The duke had been one of the few to dare correspond with the Catholic cardinal since Edward VI had proved to be such an ardent reformer. Again, Reginald wondered if his place was not at the young king's side. Would he be protecting the faith of the land or sacrificing himself?

Reginald tore into the top missive and learned that Edward was the subject at hand.

"He is dead," Reginald whispered to himself. No one else was present, but the words came anyway. "He was only a boy."

Reginald had not had a relationship with the King of England, but he had at least been safe from his wrath. Now Edward was gone, and Reginald knew exactly what he had to do - knew exactly what the rest of these letters would be urging him to do.

The devoutly Catholic Princess Mary would now be queen.

It was time for Reginald Pole to return to England.

Afterword

The reconciliation that Reginald Pole spent so much of his life hoping for and striving toward never happened. When he and Queen Mary died on November 17, 1558, the Counter-Reformation in England came to an end. To this day, Catholics and Protestants, who have splintered into many varied denominations, remain divided on justification and other important tenets of faith.

Reginald Pole almost became pope. Many thought he should wed Mary Tudor and become England's king. He succeeded, however, in his only ambition. He was a faithful follower of God.

He never finished his book on Cicero.

Cardinal Gian Pietro Carafa, whose venom likely kept Reginald from becoming pope, himself was elected in 1555. As Pope Paul IV, Carafa led harshly with no desire for reconciliation. He declared all Protestants heretics and reigns of all Protestant rulers illegitimate. During Queen Mary's reign, he ordered the return of all property confiscated during the Dissolution of the Monasteries, a task Mary could not have hoped to achieve even if she had wanted to. Carafa also ordered Reginald Pole back to Rome to stand against charges of heresy. Mary refused to send him. Pope Paul IV died on August 18, 1559.

You can read about Reginald Pole's time in England and his rise to Archbishop of Canterbury in *Queen of Martyrs: The Story of Mary I*.

Additional Reading

For those interested in reading more about the historical figures featured in this novel, I recommend the following sources:

Reginald Pole: Prince and Prophet by Thomas Mayer

The Life of Reginald Pole by Martin Haile

The Works and Writings of Reginald Pole

Michelangelo and the English Martyrs by Anne Dillon

Renaissance Woman: The Extraordinary Life and World of Vittoria Colonna by Ramie Targoff

Author's Note

I was somewhat reluctant to write about Reginald Pole. Having built a series around women's stories, I was unsure how my readers would feel about peering into a man's world. However, the more I read about Reginald, the more intrigued I became, and I was helpless to deny his story.

This, of course, is only a portion of it. Reginald's story began with his mother in *Faithful Traitor: The Story of Margaret Pole* and continues in *Queen of Martyrs: The Story of Mary I*.

What Reginald does have in common with the women I have written about is that he is something of an unsung hero. Had he placed his own ambition above his love of God, he could have been Pope or King of England. It is a testament to what type of man he was that he chose not to be either one.

Instead, he chose to be a loyal friend to fellow cardinals and artists alike, a vital councilor to his cousin, Queen Mary, and a part of the movement to reconcile Catholics and Protestants. I do believe Margaret would be proud.

Samantha Wilcoxson

Made in the USA
Middletown, DE
25 October 2022

13524906R00165